I0732566

ENDLESS

A STEEL DEMONS MC EPILOGUE

CRYSTAL ASH

Copyright © 2021 by Crystal Ash

Cover Art by MoorBooks Design

Published by Voluspa Press

This is a work of fiction. Names, characters, places, and incidents either are the products of the author's imagination or are used fictitiously. Any resemblance to actual persons, living or dead, businesses, companies, events, or locales is entirely coincidental.

All rights reserved. No part of this publication may be reproduced, distributed, or transmitted in any form or by any means, including photocopying, recording, or other electronic or mechanical methods, without the prior written permission of the publisher, except in the case of brief quotations embodied in critical reviews and certain other noncommercial uses permitted by copyright law.

SDMC series playlist

All American Nightmare - Hinder
Notorious - Adelitas Way
Hail to the King - Avenged Sevenfold
O Death - Ashley H
Joan of Arc - In This Moment
Radioactive - Imagine Dragons
Bad Company - Five Finger Death Punch
Love Me to Death - No Resolve
(Don't Fear) The Reaper - HIM
David - Noah Gunderson
Apocalyptic - Halestorm
Blue on Black - Five Finger Death Punch
Machine Gun Blues - Social Distortion
Wanted Dead or Alive - Chris Daughtry
I Get Off - Halestorm
You Shook Me All Night Long - AC/DC
Nobody Praying for Me - Seether
Loyal to No One - Dropkick Murpheys
Crazy in Love - Daniel De Bourg
Be Free - King Dude & Chelsea Wolfe
Raise Hell - Dorothy
Coming Home - Skylar Grey

Listen on Spotify at:
crystalashbooks.com/sdmc-playlist

ONE

MARIPOSA

"Congratulations, *Doctor* Mariposa Wilder!"

The smile on my face stretched into a joyful grin as I walked across the stage. I was excited for the diploma I was about to receive, certainly. But my joy was primarily due to the shouts and cheers from my family in the audience.

Jandro and Gunner were the loudest, naturally. They hooted and hollered with their best attempts to embarrass me, which made everyone in attendance laugh uproariously.

All four of my husbands stood in the front row. My parents, Reaper's parents, Noelle, Larkan, their two children, plus our closest friends in and out of the SDMC, took up the seats next to and behind my men. All of them stood, clapping and cheering. For a moment, I felt bad for the people sitting farther back, here to support the other graduates.

But nothing sent my heart soaring higher than my twin five-year-olds shouting, "Doctor Mommy!" from atop their fathers' shoulders.

Our daughter, Aurora May, sat on Gunner's shoulders. She was his spitting image, from the mass of golden curls to her permanent smile and daredevil personality. Her eyes were green instead of blue, however, which made me wonder if Reaper's DNA played any part in creating her. It wasn't possible, in the strictly scientific sense. But her fathers and I had saved this territory from the impossible years ago, so I wasn't about to completely rule it out.

Our son, Daren Javier, watched me from Shadow's shoulders. He couldn't be more different from Aurora, to the point where some couldn't believe they shared a womb. Daren was all quietness and observation to Aurora's sunshiny boisterousness. His hair and eyes were dark, lips always pressed together like he was deep in thought.

Except for now. He and his sister smiled and screamed in excitement as I accepted my diploma from Dr. Brooks.

"Congratulations, Mari." Dr. Brooks beamed as he shook my hand and pulled me close for a kiss on the cheek. "So proud of you, Doctor."

"Thank you," I whispered back through elated tears, wrapping my friend and mentor in a hug. "Couldn't have done it without you."

"Nah." He pulled away to grin at me. "You were a doctor from the very beginning."

I returned to my seat to let the ceremony continue. We were the first medical school graduates of Four Corners, a small class of twelve. Five of us were women. It had been a rigorous training program, and next year's graduating class was already double the size. Most of my class already had jobs lined up in nearby territories or here in Four Corners.

Our little home was growing faster than construction crews could keep up with. People felt safe enough to start having children, and more families migrated here every day.

Already I was excited for more patients to care for, friends for my children to play with. I still woke up some mornings, sandwiched between all of my husbands, and pinched myself. Or I started looking for my battle medic jumpsuit before remembering we no longer had a war to fight. Only much to celebrate.

My family waited for me at the side of the stage once the ceremony was over. The twins hugged my legs while their fathers smothered me in kisses. I lifted Aurora, who we nicknamed Rori, much to Reaper's dismay, into my arms, while someone else shoved a bouquet of flowers into the crook of my free arm.

"Mommy, I made you this!" Rori shoved a construction paper drawing in my face. It looked like me in my white doctor's coat, with DOCTOR MOMMY in her crayon scrawl right above it.

"Thank you, sweetie! I love it so much." I kissed her while tucking the drawing into my bouquet. "Where did everyone go?" I looked over her mass of curls to see only my husbands standing around, the auditorium cleared of everyone else.

"They went to the house to finish setting up," Jandro answered, now holding Daren against his side.

"Setting up what?"

Reaper laughed in answer. "You didn't think we'd pass up throwing a graduation party, did you?" Rori held her arms out to him, so I passed her over and he hoisted her against his side with a groan. "I got you, sugar cube."

"We just had a party," I reminded him.

"That was for completing your finals," Gunner said. "And it was like a month ago, so we were due for another one anyway."

I laughed. "It was three weeks ago!"

"You deserve another party, regardless." Shadow's hand rested on my waist, turning me toward him for a kiss. "We're so proud of you, lover."

I leaned into him, melting against his solid body. Aside from the war, medical school had been one of the toughest, most grueling experiences of my life. He and the others supporting me had made all the difference in the world.

"I have the best family that helped me get here." I held my arms out to Jandro so I could take Daren from him.

"Is there cake at home?" Daren asked me with adorable seriousness.

"Yes, son." Gunner leaned down and kissed the top of his head. "Auntie Tess and Andrea made a cake."

When Andrea and Tess got married, they insisted on making their own wedding cake, which opened up a love of baking and cake decorating for the two of them. They opened their bakery three years ago. It was down the street from Shadow's tattoo shop and a block away from Jandro's mechanic shop.

"Cake?" Rori screeched from Reaper's arms.

"Indoor voice," Reaper reminded her gently. Our running joke was that she was born without volume control. "Yes, there's cake. But lunch food first."

She tried again. "A *little* cake first?"

Reaper let out a dramatic sigh, already caving to her demands. "What does Doctor Mommy think?"

"One bite of cake before lunch." I booped Rori's nose. "Because it's my graduation."

"Me too?" Daren asked hopefully.

"Yes, you too, my boy."

Once my son got his assurance of cake, he started squirming in my arms. "Down," he grunted. He was getting to the age where he didn't want to be held by Mom, especially around others, and preferred walking on his own.

"Alright, big guy, but I'm holding your hand."

We walked out of the auditorium together with

Reaper leading the way and Jandro at his side, Gunner next to me and Daren, and Shadow bringing up the rear. Small habits like these were the hardest to change.

Several of my fellow graduates were milling about outside in the early afternoon sun, taking photos with family members or chatting excitedly amongst each other. I posed with a few of them while Jandro brought the car around, a military-grade SUV he had inspected with a fine-toothed comb and custom-fitted with extra safety features for the kids.

Naturally, all of my husbands had balked at my suggestion of a minivan.

We piled in and took the short drive home, with a few of my classmates following us. Our home had become known as the party house, and we always invited everyone. Dogs, people, and cars were already crowding our driveway, which meant the inside and backyard were already packed.

"Hades!" Rori pressed her face to the window at the sight of the big Doberman on the porch and started fumbling with the door handle.

"Hey." Shadow reached over the seat and pulled her back from the door. "Don't open that until the car's stopped."

"I wasn't," Rori whined, sitting back with a pout.

While the five of us each had our own idea of leniency and strictness with the kids, Shadow definitely veered into overprotective territory. His life experiences made him never want our children to suffer so much as a scratch. The rest of us had to occasionally reassure him it was normal for a kid to fall or scrape themselves sometimes. It was how they grew and learned their own body's limits.

The moment the car stopped, Rori was out and running up the driveway like she hadn't seen Hades in weeks. He got up and loped over to her in return, tongue lolling out in a lazy smile and stubby tail going crazy over his favorite tiny human.

The rest of us stepped out, and the smell of barbecue had my stomach growling. I hadn't eaten before the ceremony this morning because of nerves. Now that weight had lifted and I could kick back with beer, food, and my favorite people for the rest of the day.

"Oh my God, who did this?" I gasped in surprise at the "Congratulations Mari & med school grads" banner hung between the living room and kitchen. The letters looked hand-painted and included small handprints around the borders that could have only been from the kids.

"We did!" My and Reaper's moms emerged from the kitchen, each with a half-drunk mimosa in hand and a full one held out to me. The two of them had become best friends over the years and were always doing arts and crafts projects together.

"I should have known," I laughed, hugging them both and accepting the drink, taking a quick sip before pushing it back into my mom's hand. "Hold that for me. Let me get out of this gown and get some food."

"Oh, I think the boys already made a plate for you." Lis turned around and yelled toward the backyard, "Finn, Javi! Mari's home, is her food ready?"

"I've been eating off her plate," my dad teased back. "Finn's marinade is just too good."

"There's plenty of it." Finn's eyes were narrowed in concentration as he manned *two* other grills with all the seriousness of a drill sergeant.

"Jandro, go help them out back!" I yelled, heading upstairs to hang my graduation cap and gown in the bedroom closet.

A few years back, we'd done some renovation to turn the whole upper level into a bedroom for us. After the war, it was rare that any of us wanted to sleep alone. Lis knew a woodworker who'd made a bed large enough to fit all five of us comfortably. The downstairs rooms had turned into bedrooms for the kids and some private areas, like Shadow's drawing studio.

I quickly smoothed out the dress I had on under my gown, stuck my feet into comfortable sandals, and came back to join the party.

"There she is." Reaper waited for me at the bottom of the stairs, my drink and plate of food in his hands, a cocky smirk on his lips.

"Thank you, Mr. President." I reached on tiptoes

to kiss him before taking my stuff. He caught my lips with his teeth, prolonging the kiss and holding me in place with a sting of sensitivity that made a trail through my clit and down to my toes.

"Thank me again later, Mrs. President," he rumbled when he released me, eyes lighting up with a dark promise.

"Hm." I took a sip of mimosa. "I will if you don't pass out on me first, Daddy."

He laughed, following me into the kitchen with a hand on my waist. "Yeah, we'll see about that."

Even with parenting duties split up five ways, uninterrupted sleep had become a thing of the past. The kids were better at sleeping through the night now, but during parties, it was inevitable that at least one of us passed out before all the guests left. Usually it was Gunner or Reaper. About a third of the time, it was me.

Maybe it was less to do with parenting and more with getting older.

Sure enough, after hours of eating, drinking, laughing, and playing with the kids, my eyelids were drooping, and it wasn't even completely dark outside. Reaper ended up passing out on the couch as people started to leave. Someone drunkenly suggested drawing dicks on his face, and Jandro could *not* pass up that opportunity. Thankfully, he used one of the kids' washable markers instead of anything more permanent.

Jandro's face was a grimace of concentration, trying not to laugh or breathe too loudly, lest Reaper wake up. He dragged the blue marker tip over Reaper's cheek in slow, careful precision, even holding an arm out to keep Daren from getting too close when our son became curious.

"Papi, what are you drawing on Daddy's face?"

"It's a mushroom, *mijo.*"

"Why are you drawing a mushroom on his face?"

"You'll understand when you're older."

When the last guest left, Rori was curled up in the large armchair and nodding off. "Come on, Ror-meister." Shadow swept her up, carrying her off to get ready for bed. "Let's get your teeth brushed and pajamas on. What book do you want to read before bed?"

I suppressed several yawns as I tidied up the house while the guys got the kids ready for bed. When Reaper rolled groggily off the couch, I tried to hide my laughter but knew it wouldn't last long. He came up behind me while I washed dishes and I held my breath.

"Stop. Leave that for the morning and we'll get it." Reaper wrapped me up in a sensual hug, oblivious to the mark on his face. He had cut way back on smoking and didn't smell of cloves so strongly anymore. But his hug enveloped me in that familiar leather and whiskey scent that I wouldn't trade for the world.

"…Kay." My shoulders shook from how hard I was trying to keep it in.

"Sugar? What is it?" His eyes narrowed.

"You should," I suppressed a snort, covering my mouth, "look in the mirror."

He released me to stomp down the hallway, and I couldn't hold back any longer. Peals of laughter broke from my mouth, and then tears sprung to my eyes when I heard, "JANDRO, WHAT THE FUCK!" reverberate through the house.

"Relax, it's washable," Jandro called from Daren's room.

"It fuckin' better be!"

I went to bed exhausted but still giggling. Just another day of being married to four Steel Demons.

TWO

MARIPOSA

———

The bedroom was bright when I woke up. My eyes cracked open to find a glass of water and ibuprofen tablets on the nightstand. I scooted toward the edge to take them, mindful of the heavy, scarred arm draped over my waist.

Once I swallowed the tablets and drained the water, I retreated to the cocoon of warmth at my back, and the surrounding arm tightened protectively.

"Good morning," Shadow mumbled, his breath soft on the back of my neck.

"Morning, love." I peeked over and behind him to see that we were alone in bed. A rare moment.

"How are you feeling, Doctor?" I heard the smile in his sleepy voice and felt it in the kiss he brushed over my shoulder.

"Pretty good, just a little headache." I rubbed my temple where the ache was already starting to fade.

"Not bad for losing track of my mimosas yesterday." I looked back to kiss the scar on his brow. "How do you feel?"

"Oh, fine. I only had a couple."

Shadow had cut his drinking back to almost nothing since I'd been pregnant with the twins. He didn't drink at all most days now and only indulged a little when we threw parties. He said it was because he wanted to be present at all times for the kids. Not that he was *ever* unaware of his surroundings, but since becoming a dad, he took hypervigilance to a whole new level.

I wiggled my ass on his morning wood to tease him, earning a throaty groan for my effort. "You're allowed to let loose, you know."

"I did," he protested, clamping a hand down on my hip to still me. "I had fun. And it was good to see *you* let loose before you start official doctor duties."

I reached back, threading my fingers through his long black hair to find purchase on his neck. "I'm glad you had fun."

"I always do when you and the kids are happy."

The smile I wore threatened to split my face. My chest sparked and fluttered as I spun in his arms to face him. Even after nearly a decade together, these men spurred these reactions in me. If anything, my love for them ran deeper now than when we were in the thick of war together.

Shadow kissed me deeply, pressing me down into

the mattress as we lazily rolled together. We knew each other's bodies so well now. I had kissed every scar on him hundreds of times over, had him permanently mapped out and imprinted in my mind. He had only grown more attentive and loving as years passed. The violence had bled out of him long before he held our twins for the first time, leaving behind one of the most devoted fathers and husbands I'd ever seen.

Shadow's mouth fell to my neck, his strong thighs nudging my legs apart so he could settle between them, when a thumping at the bedroom door startled us both.

"Mommy!" Rori yelled from the other side, palm insistently slapping the door. "Mommy, wake up!"

Shadow inhaled sharply as he lifted away, but before either of us could say anything, we heard Gunner coming up the stairs. "Hey, what are you doing? Mommy's sleeping. Come have breakfast."

"But I want to show her my…"

Rori's voice faded as Gunner took her back downstairs. Shadow and I held our breaths, glanced at each once, then burst into soft laughter.

"Isn't parenting everything you've ever dreamed of?" I teased, curling into his side.

"Everything and so much more," he sighed, caressing a hand down my back.

I propped my chin on his chest to look at him, my

curiosity now piqued. "Really? You were so worried in the beginning."

"I'm still worried. Every day there's something new to worry about." He flashed a sheepish smile. "At first, my worries were mostly to do with you."

"You mean, the pregnancy."

"Mmhm. Just pregnancy in general, at first. Then when we found out they were twins, well, that scared me to death."

"Me too, actually," I confessed. "I never imagined having twins. There's none in my family or anything."

"And you still wanted a natural birth," Shadow teased, playing with the ends of my hair.

"Absolutely! I mean, they were healthy, and the decision just felt right. Call it maternal instinct or whatever, but I knew it was the right way to deliver them."

"Maybe it was the divine feminine in you." Shadow brushed a kiss across my forehead. "The aspect of Freyja that's part of you."

Something clicked into place when he said that. I hadn't consciously felt the goddess since she stopped possessing my body all those years ago, but it made total sense.

"I bet you're right," I said in an awed whisper. As exhausting and uncomfortable that carrying two babies had been, it had been a surprisingly easy pregnancy. My water broke at just past thirty-seven weeks, which was considered full-term for twins. Daren came into the world first, and Rori followed four minutes later. They were small, as twins tended to be, but absolutely perfect. The guys and I rushed to the hospital in the early morning and came home with our children that same evening.

"Once they were born, and I knew you were okay," Shadow went on. "That made room for a whole slew of new worries to pop up."

"Because they were our fragile, precious, screaming, pooping infants we were all now responsible for keeping alive?"

"That was part of it." Shadow's wry smile faded, and he went quiet.

I snuggled into him, peppering kisses on his neck and running light caresses over him to reassure him. "What else?"

He hesitated a moment longer before answering. "That if either of them were biologically mine, the possibility that they might've…inherited something from me." At my narrow-eyed stare, he elaborated. "Or from my mother, or father, even. I don't know what that would be exactly, but something bad."

"Shadow." I returned my head to his chest, wrapping both arms around him. "Love, we ran those genetic tests, remember? Everything came back normal."

"I know, but I don't mean something physically wrong. Like, I was born physically normal. So was my mother, I'm sure. But neither of us ended up that way."

"Hey, listen." I lifted my cheek to look at him again. "You're not defective in any way. You never were." I found one of his hands and laced my fingers through his. "Everything you've struggled with was because of the environment you were in, not because there was anything inherently wrong with you."

"But we don't know that for sure." Shadow placed an arm behind his head, his expression thoughtful. "I never had a normal environment to compare it to. For all we know, I could have turned out the same."

"What about now?" I challenged. "And the last several years? You've been an amazing husband and father. You're the most sought-after tattoo artist in the Southwest, with a year-long wait list. Our children love you." I leaned in to hover my lips over his. "*I* love you."

His smile finally returned before the distance between our lips closed. "I love you so much. And you're right. These past few years have been just… perfect. Having you as my wife every day." He stroked tenderly over my cheek. "Watching the kids grow. Seeing the tattoo shop become what it is. I never could have imagined this before."

I let my forehead touch his, soaking up this moment of reflection with him. Every once in a while, the guys and I would have moments like these.

Usually after the kids went to bed and when other things didn't need our immediate attention.

This beautiful little family, this amazing life we had—we could never forget how hard we fought for this. We nearly destroyed ourselves and each other before we made it here, and we'd never take it for granted.

"The kids will only inherit the best things from you," I said after a few moments of quiet. "They've already gotten started. Daren is drawing nonstop and Rori," I grinned at him, "she's your little shadow."

"She is." Shadow's smile grew even broader at the mention of our daughter. "I don't know how that happened. She's so much like Gunner, and with Reaper's bossiness."

I couldn't help but laugh at how true that was, sliding off of Shadow to land next to him on the mattress. "Speaking of, ready to get up and see what she wanted to show us?"

"Yes." Shadow pushed the sheet away and swung his feet to the floor. "I'm ready for breakfast even more."

I remained in bed, just watching as he went to the dresser to pull on sweatpants and a shirt. His broad back and perky ass were every bit as delicious now as they were eight years ago. Only his scars looked softer this morning, probably because of the morning light in the bedroom.

Shadow turned around once he got dressed and

smirked when he caught me staring. Finally, the man had started to understand how attractive he was.

"Are you having some trouble getting up?" He approached the edge of the bed, his body tense and a wicked gleam in his eye.

My heart sped up with the thrill of his body language. "Um, no."

A beat of frozen silence passed before I scrambled for the opposite edge of the bed. Shadow reached over and grabbed my ankle easily, dragging me back toward him with an amused chuckle. He ignored my shrieks and playful protests, knowing full-well now that I wasn't actually trying to escape him.

Shadow trapped me easily underneath him, pinning me down with kisses and tickles until I was breathless. Then he swatted my ass and lifted away, leaving me wanting and weak-kneed, to get dressed.

JANDRO

I woke up to a package on the porch from my sister, Angie, and her husband, Drew. They mailed a bunch of Christmas gifts for the kids months ago, which we figured had gotten lost. Postal systems were still inconsistent between the different territories and unreliable at best. So it was a nice surprise to find, even if it was three months late.

The kids digging through the box and playing with their new toys allowed us three dads to wake up slowly with some coffee while Mari and Shadow slept in. They had just gotten up as I was starting breakfast for everyone.

"Smells great, Jandro." Shadow came down the stairs first, a smile still pulling on his lips from his lay-in with Mari. They hadn't gotten a lot of private time lately, with her preparing for graduation and him booked with back-to-back tattoo appointments. I was glad Reaper and Gunner followed my lead in getting up early.

Shadow was headed off at the bottom of the stairs by Rori, holding up some tiny dollhouse thing. "Dad, look what I got!"

"What did you get? Can I see?" The shift in his tone was never something I thought I'd hear. Not until he started talking to Mari over eight years ago. And now our daughter threatened to unseat her as the woman who had the most power over him.

Mari came downstairs moments later, heading straight for me. "Do you need help?"

"Not from you, Doctor." I pushed a mug of coffee into her hands with a grin and a fast kiss. "Although I might need your expertise *later*."

"Mmhm, body exam sex jokes, very funny." She smirked over the rim of her coffee cup. "You said something similar when we first met. Do you remember that?"

"Me?" I slapped a hand to my chest dramatically. "Saying innuendos to a beautiful girl I was hoping to sleep with? That doesn't sound like me at all."

"You said it to all the girls then," Mari teased with a playful glare.

"But I wifed up the best one." I squeezed her shoulders and planted a kiss on her forehead. "Sit down, see what Angie sent the kids. I'll bring you breakfast." I followed her out to the living room just to snap a towel at Gunner's head. "Get in here and help."

"Jesus, fine. Be right back, little dude." He and Reaper were going through smaller boxes of Legos with our son, Daren.

"Can you handle pancakes?" I shoved the bowl of batter at Gunner. "Don't burn them."

"Fuck yeah, pancakes!" He got to stirring excitedly.

"Little ones for the kids. No bigger than a softball."

"I know dude, I got it." He poured the batter with surprising care, making explosion noises that got Daren all excited from the living room.

Dad-life had infected Gunner with a childlike excitement about all the little things. He was the fun dad, for sure. Me? I considered myself the teacher. I took every opportunity I could to show the kids how something worked, whether it was cooking or the bubbles in their bath. Shadow was the neurotic, over-protective one, although he was getting better at dialing it back. Reaper, oddly enough, turned out to be the most well-balanced of us.

While Gunner poured, flipped, and stacked pancakes, I worked on the eggs and bacon. The aroma started filling up the house and Gun's curious little miniature wandered in to investigate.

"Listo para comer, mijita?" I asked Rori if she was

ready to eat as she wandered to my side of the counter. "Not too close, baby. It's hot."

"Papi, can I have an egg?" She stood on tiptoes, grabbing drawer handles like she was ready to climb up and swipe the whole pan of scrambled eggs for herself.

I touched her chin to bring her attention to me. *"En español, mijita."* She knew the words, she just needed to practice saying them. There was always a teachable moment.

Rori frowned, the frustration settling into her tightly-knitted eyebrows. "I don't know how." Her voice was climbing into that whine, the one that preceded all her worst tantrums.

This was the other side to always wanting to teach them something, dealing with the impatience and struggles when they didn't succeed right away. But not everything would come easily to them, and they had to learn that too.

Thankfully, it was Reaper to the rescue.

"Yes, you do." He crouched low next to her, hugging one arm around her waist. "I'll help you. We'll say it together, okay?" Rori's attention was successfully diverted to him, a welcome distraction from her tantrum. She watched his mouth intently, mimicking him as he slowly formed the words.

"Un…"

"Un…"

"Hue…"

"H-h-hue…"

"*Hue-vito*. You got it, sugar cube."

"*Un hue-vito.*" Rori turned back to me. "*Por favor.*"

Only a completely heartless bastard would not have melted at the look my daughter gave me right then. All the times I got shot up and nearly died, when I thought I lost Mari and everyone else—it was worth it for that look alone.

"Very good, *mijita.*" I composed myself fast enough to scoop her up, tucking her against my side as I planted a big kiss on her cheek. "You're so smart, and I'm proud of you." I kissed her other cheek. "I love you."

I made a mental note to let her know how proud I was as often as possible. While Four Corners was relatively safe, it could be generations before the outside world was as safe for girls as it once was. Wherever my daughter ended up in her adult life, I wanted her to feel confident in how intelligent she was. I never wanted her to doubt for a second that she was loved.

"*Huevito!*" Rori repeated insistently.

"Yeah, yeah. I got your eggs right here, princess." I scooped up a spoonful of scrambled egg that had already cooled next to the stove and held it up to her lips. "Test it for me. Is it ready?"

She took the biggest bite possible off the end of the wooden spoon and proceeded to spill small crumbles of egg onto the floor. Good thing Hades was there to clean it all up.

"How is it? Good?" At her enthusiastic nod, I put her spoon aside and handed her a clean one. "Help me stir this next batch. It's almost ready. Hey!" My head whipped around at the sight of Reaper in my periphery. "Fuck off, bacon thief!"

"What?" Reaper unashamedly fed the strip of meat to Hades, who inhaled it. "He can't have eggs without bacon."

"Fuck off!" Rori parroted me, waving the stirring spoon at Reaper.

"I love you too, sugar cube." Reaper took the spoon from her and kissed her forehead.

We tried not to swear in front of the kids at first, we really did. But even Mari slipped sometimes, despite being the biggest enforcer of it. The kids' teachers didn't approve, obviously, but in the end, we decided it wasn't all that harmful. If anything, a bigger vocabulary was a good thing, right? Especially if they learned to speak two languages.

"Alright, I'm putting you down." I placed Rori carefully on the floor, then turned the burners off. "Have a seat and I'll bring you a plate, *mijita*."

We got the kids seated with food, an endeavor that went smoothly this morning, before getting ourselves plated up.

"Thank you, *guapito*." Mari kissed me as she breezed past me in the kitchen.

I smacked her ass before she could dodge out of

the way. "My pleasure." And it really was. Taking care of my family was all I'd ever wanted to do.

The kids were hungry, but they were eager to get back to their box of toys, so they inhaled their food and squirmed in their seats.

"Slow down, child. You'll get a tummy ache." Mari wiped pancake syrup and crumbled egg from Rori's mouth. "Drink some juice."

"Papi, papi. Can you help me..."

"Finish chewing your food, son," I reminded Daren. "Yes, what can I help you with?"

"Can you help me build a... a motorcycle with the Legos I got from Uncle Drew?"

My chest swelled up so much when he asked that question, I thought it would burst. I had secretly hoped that at least one of my kids would want to build and tinker with stuff. Of course, I wanted them to pursue their own interests and not force them into anything, but I fantasized about working on projects with my son or daughter. Being able to teach them hands-on about mechanics and how things worked was a dream. One that my son just brought to reality with his innocent question.

"You want me to help you build a motorcycle?" My five-year-old had no idea what this meant to me, but all the adults in attendance did. Mari beamed at me from across the table and the guys let out soft, approving chuckles.

"Yeah! There's wheels and a bunch of other little parts, but I don't know where they go."

"Don't worry." I ruffled his dark hair, which was in thick, soft waves like Mari's, and kissed the top of his head. "We'll build you a bitchin' ride. But finish your breakfast first."

Daren wolfed down the rest of his eggs and bacon before politely asking to be excused.

He bolted to the living room coffee table just as his sister was finishing up.

"Rori, do you want to build motorcycles with Daren?" Mari teased our daughter, clearing plates from the table.

"No. Daddy, can I have tattoos?" Rori peered up at Shadow, grabbing his forearm that depicted Mari as a sexy pin-up girl.

"Again?" He smiled at her, pinching her cheek playfully. "You washed off your tattoos in the bath the other day."

"I want flowers this time. Like Mommy's. Oh, and I want a cat! Like Freyja."

"What do you say?"

"Pleeease!"

Shadow slid a glance over to Mari before giving in. "Alright. But they're getting washed off again before you go back to school."

"Her teacher just has a massive stick up her ass," Gunner declared, shoving the last big bite of pancake into her mouth.

"Gun." Mari smacked his arm but had giggled despite the chastisement.

"You know I'm right, baby girl. She said 'shit' *one* time—"

"It was 'bullshit' actually," Reaper chuckled. "I picked her up that day, and yes, her teacher was very concerned about how she expressed that the coloring project was bullshit."

"That's our girl," I laughed, collecting the rest of the dishes.

"And then the teacher came at me when *I* picked her up," Shadow continued. "Because Rori was showing off her 'tattoos' to the rest of the class. I had to explain to this lady that it was washable marker."

"She thinks we're raising degenerates." Reaper crunched his bacon with a satisfied smirk.

"All this is telling me is Rori's the coolest kid in her class," Gunner concluded.

"And thank everything that Daren is polite and sweet and *quiet*," Mari punctuated the last word with a soft laugh. "Because I could not handle two Roris."

"Speaking of." I rinsed off my hands in the sink and dried them on a towel. "If anyone needs me, I'll be building a motorcycle with my son."

Fuck, it felt so damn good to say that.

FOUR

SHADOW

"How've you been, big man?" Declan removed his shirt and folded it neatly on a chair before lying down on my tattoo bench. "You look good."

"Thanks. I've been great, actually." I pulled on my gloves and wheeled up next to him on my stool, bringing my cart of supplies along behind me. "Business is good. I got a family now."

"Good for you, man." He turned his head toward the shelf on the wall of my tattoo shop. "Is that them right there?"

I followed his gaze to the framed picture of Mari and the twins, taken just last week at her graduation party. Mari was holding Rori, the two of them smiling brightly while Daren stood next to his mom and clung to her hip, his expression more shy and withdrawn.

"Yeah." I cleaned Declan's skin with antiseptic while my chest did that elated flipping sensation. It

29

never ceased to amaze me that my entire world was in that picture. And that it was real. "That's my wife and our twins."

"Beautiful." Declan looked away from the wall and relaxed while I began to sketch over his chest in pen.

"This has held up well," I remarked on the dragon's head on the right side of his chest, which I had done for him in prison around eighteen years ago. It was the first expansive tattoo I'd ever done, starting at his chest, then winding over his shoulder and down his back. I'd poked it entirely by hand over a period of several weeks. It looked rougher than my current style, but not as bad as I expected. I could sharpen up the lines easily, then add the color he wanted.

"Told you it still looked good." Declan grinned. "I'm not surprised at all that you're running a shop now. You always did good work."

"Thanks. I couldn't believe that was you walking outside. You bulked up, kid."

"So did you, man!" He laughed. "I didn't know whether to hug you when I saw you or run away shitting my pants."

"You never gave me a hard time," I said. "If you had been one of the guards, it might be a different story."

I finished the sketch and got his approval on it, then proceeded to start the real inking.

"Are you staying in Four Corners?" I asked between the buzzes of my machine.

"Ah, I'm kind of all over the place." A dismissive answer, but I didn't pry. We had been acquaintances but not especially friendly. I never learned why he ended up in prison, especially so young. He'd been a wide-eyed teenager back then, thrown into a cage with some of the worst criminals in the world.

I was lucky that Jandro took me in with the Demons once the inmates started rioting and breaking out. In all likelihood, Declan was not as lucky.

"I'm spending a lot of time in Blakeworth these days," he continued after a brief pause.

"Blakeworth?" I couldn't hide my surprise. He was definitely not part of their elite class, which was still struggling after we kicked their asses, despite their best efforts to save face. We continue to see propaganda coming out of there saying that their wealth and prosperity were at an all-time high because they beat *us* in that last battle. A bald-faced lie to their own citizens, and a shitty one at that.

"My line of work is…not entirely legal." I felt Declan's eyes on me as I touched up spots on his dragon and knew he was gauging my reaction.

"As long as you're not trafficking people, I won't judge what you do," I informed him.

He relaxed, taking a big breath. "Nah, nothing like that. I'm a cage fighter."

"Really?" That surprised me too, but not in a bad way. "So getting scrappy in the yard turned out to be useful for you, huh?"

"You could say that," he laughed. "It's all underground up there. The fancy doodads made laws against it, but some of them come to every fight and they love to gamble. It's very few rules, bare fists and shit. And *huge* fuckin' payouts."

"Yeah? What's your record?"

Declan grinned broadly. "I'm undefeated."

"No shit." I was oddly fascinated. As an assassin, I wouldn't make for a very entertaining fighter. But if I hadn't ended up with the Demons, I may have found myself doing very similar work. Although my socially stunted ass would've most likely ended up in a gladiator type of situation.

"Yeah, you should come see me fight sometime. Might want to leave the wife and kids at home, though. It gets pretty brutal."

I paused to sit up and stretch my hand, returning his grin. "I would, but I'm pretty sure I'll be arrested on sight if I ever show my face in Blakeworth again."

"For real?" Declan's eyes widened. "Okay, I need to hear *that* story."

We spent the next few hours swapping war stories while I tattooed him. All the line work on his dragon became sharp and crisp. I had started adding shading to the surrounding smoke, plus green and gold coloring to the dragon's scales, when we decided to stop.

"I'll be in town 'til the end of the week." Declan sat up from the bench after I cleaned his skin and went to grab his shirt. Now that I knew what to look for, he clearly moved like a fighter. "Thanks for squeezing me in, Shadow. I know you're busy as hell these days."

"It's no trouble. I actually keep my schedule pretty flexible in case something comes up with the kids." Speaking of, it was my day to pick up Rori from school. I cleaned up my area quickly, not wanting to leave a mess for my shop apprentice. "Come by in the mornings," I told Declan. "I have to pick up my daughter, but tomorrow I can work on you for an hour longer."

"Sounds good, Shadow. We'll catch up more over a drink later, yeah?"

"Sure. See you, Dec."

———

"AND THEN WE PLAYED TAG, and I was It, but *guess what*, Dad!"

"What happened, Ror?" I held on to my daughter's hand as we walked up the driveway together, carrying her llama backpack in the other hand. Ever since we went on a family trip to an alpaca farm a few weeks ago, she'd been obsessed with llamas and alpacas.

"I tagged everyone!" Rori released my hand and started jumping and skipping in front of me. "'Cause I'm the fastest! I was like this!" She sprinted up the rest of the driveway to the front door, where Hades waited for her on the front porch.

"Wow, look at you go!" I dug out my keys, smiling at my exuberant daughter. *That's one way to burn all that energy.*

The dog matched her excitement, returning her tackling hug with face licks and excited tail-wagging as I let us into the house.

"Hades, can you catch me?" Rori darted through the living room, circling the couches with her bright laughter as Hades chased her.

"Hey Freyja." I set our stuff down and greeted the sleepy cat with an ear scratch. She head-butted my hand once, then promptly turned around to sleep in a different position. "Fair enough, we'll hang out when it's quieter."

Freyja loved Rori, but didn't care for our daughter's tendency to tornado around the house when she was at full energy.

Playing tag at school seemed to drain her earlier than usual, though. Hades only chased her for a few minutes before she sprawled out on the couch, panting.

"Do you want a snack, Ror-meister?" We had the

house to ourselves until the others got home, so the kitchen was unusually quiet and empty without Jandro whipping up something.

"Yes, please. Can I have animal crackers?"

"Sure. Drink some water for me, okay? You ran a lot today."

"Okay."

I set out her snack for her, then flipped through some upcoming tattoo sketches while Rori nibbled her crackers. Declan wanted a lion on his back, interacting somehow with the dragon once I finished adding color to the scales. I got so absorbed in sketching that I didn't notice Rori had finished her snack until she crawled up on the couch and nestled into my side.

"What are you drawing, Daddy?" She leaned on my shoulder, voice quiet and calm.

"Some tattoos for work." I brought an arm around her and dropped a kiss to her forehead. "What do you think of this lion?"

"He's hungry. He's gonna bite the snake." She pointed to where the lion's open jaws hovered dangerously close to the back end of the dragon.

"That's a dragon, silly." I tugged a lock of her hair. "See? He's scaly like a snake, but he has feet."

"Where are his wings?" Rori's eyelids blinked heavily. All that running around really tuckered her out today.

"This one doesn't have wings, but he does breathe

fire." I flipped to another page where I had drawn the details of the dragon's head. "See all this smoke coming out of his mouth? And he's got feet up here too, so he's got four legs."

Rori shifted into my side and curled her legs up until she was a small ball. If she was getting comfortable for a nap, I'd be stuck here and have zero complaints about it. The others warned me our kids would want to spend a lot less time with us as they got older. I already couldn't believe how fast the last five years had flown by, so I was more than happy to cherish these moments with them.

"Falling asleep on me, Ror-meister?" I set aside the sketchbook and shifted to a more comfortable position while trying not to disturb her.

"No…" Her eyelids batted open, green eyes focusing on my arm around her. One small hand reached out, skimming over my years upon years of scar tissue. "You got so many owies, Daddy."

I tensed, and my heart started to race. I knew the kids would notice and ask questions at some point, but still felt completely unprepared for this moment. How much, if anything, should I tell her? Especially at this age?

"It's okay. They don't hurt anymore, sweetheart. They're really old." I tapped a finger to her nose. "Much older than you."

"But you got *a lot*. Like seventy-million." She followed the map of crisscrossing lines up my arm with her fingers, taking in how extensive they were. "I know! I'll kiss them better."

I just sat back, stunned, as my daughter placed messy kisses all over my arm, something she must have picked up from her mother. Mari kissed the kids' band-aids whenever they got a cut or scrape, then declared them all better before wrapping them up in a hug. Her doing that seemed to soothe and comfort them more than the actual treatment of the wound. And now my daughter was doing it to me.

"All better!" Rori wrapped her arms around my neck and smacked a kiss on my cheekbone. "You're okay now, Daddy."

Okay was the understatement of the year. I was a completely different person since she'd come into my life. Sure, my arm was now covered in drool, but fuck if I was ever going to wipe it off. I hugged my sweet, beautiful daughter and forced words out through the emotion tightening my throat.

"Thank you, sweetheart. I'm so, *so* much better now."

———

THE CLICK of the front door unlocking roused me from sleep. My attention was split between Rori, dead asleep on my chest, and Mari entering the house.

"Hi guys—oh!" She lowered her voice to a

whisper as I brought a finger to my lips. "Hi. How did you get her to fall asleep?"

"Playing tag at school," I whispered back. We shared a quick kiss before Mari went to change out of her work clothes while I carefully lifted up from the couch, carrying Rori to her room to finish her nap. Mari was nibbling one of Rori's ignored animal crackers when I returned. "How was work?" I pulled her close by the waist for a proper kiss.

"Good." She raised on tiptoes and leaned the length of her body on me through our kiss. "Two more confirmed pregnancies with twins! I'm telling you, there's some fertility mojo in the air."

Freyja hopped down from her sleeping spot right then, greeting Mari with a meow and a rub around her ankles.

"Yes, is this your doing?" Mari picked up the cat and flipped her belly up. "Anything you'd like to tell me?"

Freyja stared back blankly, pupils wide. We still talked to the animals and searched for the hints of that ancient wisdom in their eyes. They never spoke again after we left New Ireland, but that didn't mean we weren't being heard.

Mari set Freyja down once the cat started squirming in protest. "How was your day, love?" Her arms went around my waist, pressing herself flush against me again.

"Good. Had a surprise walk-in from an old prison

acquaintance. He's in town temporarily, and I'll be working on him while he's here. He's safe, no trouble," I added at her tense expression.

"Ah well, that's good. Was it nice to catch up with him?"

"Yes, actually. He's doing some underground, not entirely legal work in Blakeworth." Mari didn't like fighting. She hated the Fight Nights we had back in Sheol, so I left that detail out.

She laughed softly, putting away Rori's discarded snack. "Good for him, as long as he doesn't get caught."

"I don't think he will." I went to help her wipe crumbs from the kitchen table. "Where's Daren?"

"I dropped him off at the pool with Gunner." Mari tossed a smirk at me over her shoulder. "That boy will not live to adulthood fearing water like I did. Did Rori's teacher give you any grief?"

"Not today," I answered distractedly. Her comment about Daren dredged up some worries I'd been mulling over about our son but hadn't had a chance to voice yet. "Lover, do you think Daren's okay?"

Mari paused in tidying up the kitchen, her brows furrowing together. "What do you mean?"

"He's…a little different, isn't he? Just in general."

Her expression turned thoughtful as she wandered closer to me. "He's quiet, a little shy. I haven't noticed anything wrong with him. Or do you mean something else?"

"No, it's like what you're saying. He doesn't have a lot of friends. He prefers doing things by himself, instead of playing with other kids. He doesn't get… excited about things like Rori does. I just wonder why he isolates himself like that."

"Shadow." Mari's head tilted as she looked at me, a smile growing on her face. "You know what I'm hearing?"

"No, what?"

"You're worried about our son turning out like you."

"That's not…" *Fuck. Yes, it is.*

The realization must have been clear on my face because Mari returned to standing in front of me, dragging a light touch up my chest to my neck. "Not every child can be a screaming tornado of sunshine like our daughter. Daren is his own person. If he's introverted and not the most boisterous kid in the room, that's who he is, and we should support him no matter what."

"Of course I'll support him. It's just…" It seemed so obvious now that she made that connection. My fears were rooted in my own upbringing, in the childhood I never got to have. "I worry when I see him intentionally withdraw from people. I don't want him to struggle with the same things I did as he gets older.

Before I met you, I could barely talk to anyone. I don't want that for him."

Mari's fingers dragged over my neck and scalp as she listened, the touch grounding and soothing. "Our son is loved," she said. "He's so smart, kind, and creative. He's not antisocial, he's just very…" She paused to think. "Cerebral. Daren's in his head a lot, always thinking."

"You're right. He's all of those things." I leaned my forehead on hers. "He has it so good. It's stupid of me to worry."

"No, love. I think worrying is normal." She scratched deliciously up the back of my head. "We want them to have everything we didn't have and to never experience the awful things that we went through."

"I know. But we need to give them room to be themselves too."

"I wanted to wait until everyone was home to tell you guys." Mari smiled. "But you should know that Daren's teacher told me something wonderful today."

"What? What happened?" My heart lifted at the pride shining through Mari.

"They got a new student in class, a deaf girl. You know how resources are short now, so they're not sure when she'll get an interpreter."

"These kids need their own classes, with specialized instructors, so they don't fall behind," I said with a soft growl. "It's not fair to her."

"I know, love. And she's nonverbal, plus she's new, so the other kids didn't really make an effort to play with her." Mari grinned. "Except for one."

"Daren."

Mari nodded, beaming up at me. "He sat next to her when no one else did. They communicated through pictures and notes." She snorted out a soft laugh. "Well, his best attempts at notes, anyway. That boy writes in chicken scratch."

"He did that? Unprompted?" This wasn't disbelief I was feeling. I had no doubts my son could make friends. But I wanted to hear Mari say it again and again. I wanted to see it with my own eyes, just to feel this elation and pride in him.

"He did," Mari confirmed, leaning her chest on mine as she wrapped around me tighter. "So I don't think you need to worry, love. He's quiet and solitary for a kid, but his heart is so big."

"You're right." My arms wrapped around her back, holding her to me so I could rest my cheek on top of her head. "Our kids are going to be fine."

FIVE

GUNNER

"You'd really rather sit there and kick the water instead of getting in?"

"Yeah," Daren said succinctly. He was sitting at the edge of our community pool, swimming trunks and water wings on, splashing the water with his feet, but absolutely refusing to get in.

This was our third attempt, and I was hoping it'd be the charm. But we'd been here about fifteen minutes already and no such luck.

The water was shallow at this end, barely coming up to my waist. I could sit on the bottom and still have my head above the surface. Not many people were around, just a group of friends lounging on deck chairs and a couple of lap swimmers in the deep end.

I lifted out of the water just enough to put my arms on either side of Daren. "Talk to me, son. What are you worried about?"

"I told you, drowning!" he retorted with a narrow-eyed stare at me. "And sea monsters."

I held back a chuckle. Maybe telling him bedtime stories about sirens and krakens sinking ships wasn't the best idea.

"No sea monsters in here, buddy." I leaned back, spreading my arms wide below the surface. "See? You can see all the way to the bottom across the whole pool."

"Daddy Shadow told me an octopus can camouflage themselves to look like anything. So they could just be hiding."

Damn it, Shadow.

I returned my hands to the ledge. "I promise you, there are no sea monsters here. I won't let anything happen to you, you're safe."

Years ago, I said something similar to Mari when I got her to float on her back. She barely knew me back then and trusted me anyway. I was trying not to show frustration toward my own son for not trusting me. Facing fears was different for kids, I knew that.

Daren leaned forward, peering into the pool with a scrutinizing gaze. I wondered then, as I often did, which one of us made him. Rori was obviously mine. But with Daren, it was less obvious.

He was quiet and thoughtful, like Shadow, and a hands-on learner who loved tinkering, like Jandro. Some of his physical features reminded me of Reaper and Daren, the uncle he never got to know and his namesake.

But mostly, he looked like Mari. He sure as shit inherited her fear of water.

"How about this?" I said when he seemed no closer to getting in. "Hold on to me and I'll dip you, just up to your legs. We won't even get your belly-button wet." A slower approach would probably work best for him, and I poked him in the belly to illustrate my point.

But something else had caught Daren's attention, and I followed his gaze across the pool.

A girl about his age and her mom were entering the pool area together. The girl fidgeted excitedly, her hands moving rapidly as her mother led them to an empty deck chair to set their stuff down. Her mom made some gestures with her hands and it dawned on me that they were speaking sign language.

I looked back at Daren, tickling his foot under the water to get his attention. "Who's that, bud? Do you know her?"

"That's Lily, she's my friend," he said. "She can't hear us, so we have to wait until she sees us to say hi."

"Oh, okay." I turned around again to see that Lily's mom had put goggles on her daughter's head and removed what looked like hearing aids from her ears.

The little girl looked up, and I knew immediately when she saw Daren. A big smile spread across her face, and she waved excitedly at him. Her mother caught on, and I gave a polite wave to her.

Lily snapped her goggles over her eyes, made a quick sign at Daren, then started *running* to the edge of the pool.

Oh fuck, she's going to slip and fall. I pushed away from Daren's ledge and went toward her, not thinking about how I'd tell her to be careful. I just wanted to be there to help if she got hurt.

It was all for naught, however, as Lily straightened her arms above her head, stacked her palms on top of each other, and made a smooth, perfect dive into the pool. I stopped in my tracks, utterly stunned, and I knew Daren had to be too. I'd been swimming since I could crawl, and I definitely couldn't dive like that at five years old.

"Showing off for her friend," Lily's mom laughed as she approached the pool's edge. "Hi, I'm Anna."

"I don't blame her, that was amazing." I said. "I'm Gunner, Daren's dad."

"Nice to meet you both. We're new to Four Corners, and it sounds like those two really hit it off in school today."

"I'm glad to hear it."

Lily had been frog-kicking underwater on her way to Daren's side of the pool, her head popping up just a few feet away from where he was sitting.

"Wow!" His eyes were big and round as he stared at her. "You're like a fish." He pointed at Lily, then placed his hands behind his ears to wave them like gills as he sucked his cheeks in.

Lily let out a soft sound that must have been a laugh, then signed something at Daren before beckoning him to join her in the water. He looked up at me, that same apprehension in his eyes from before. But now there was something else—determination.

"Yeah, we're still working on the whole 'getting in the pool' part." I chuckled at Anna as I made my way back over to Daren's side. Lily turned around as I approached, and I greeted her with a smile and two thumbs up. "Great dive, that was awesome!" I wasn't sure if she read lips, but made an effort to speak slowly and enunciate the words anyway.

The little girl beamed and touched her hand to her mouth, bringing her forearm down in a smooth arc.

"She says 'thanks'," Daren interpreted for me proudly. "That's my dad." He pointed at me and made another sign with his hand, spreading his fingers wide and touching his thumb to his forehead.

My chest swelled with pride. He learned quickly and was already picking up Spanish words from Jandro. When Mari's parents came over, Daren and his grandfather Javier were able to have complete, albeit simple, conversations entirely in Spanish. And now here he was, picking up a third language like it was nothing. I couldn't wait to tell the others when we got home.

"She's asking Daren to get in the pool with her." Lily's mom sat on the ledge a few feet away from my son, dipping her feet and calves into the water and signing as she spoke.

He seemed more determined to try, gripping the pool's edge in his small hands and staring down at the surface like it was his arch nemesis. I didn't want to add to the pressure he was likely already putting on himself, nor did I want to embarrass him in front of his new friend. So I moved to the side as he started to scoot, inch by inch, off the ledge.

"Do you want help, buddy?" I asked in a low voice, meant only for him to hear.

"No, I got it."

I kept my arm near him just in case, but let him be as he slowly eased more of his legs into the water. At the last moment, when he let go of the edge and hit the water with a splash, he did grab my arm with a frightened gasp. The water wings kept his shoulders and head above the surface, so he was completely safe.

I brought Daren close to me anyway, drawing him into a hug while wishing Mari could see this. "Good job, dude! I got you, you're okay."

Lily and her mom both clapped in support, which made Daren go shy and hide his face against my side.

"Aw, son, I'm proud of you." He continued to hold my arm as I lowered into the water, bringing my face level with his. "You did it! How do you feel?"

"Okay. It's not so bad." He was trying to play it cool in front of the ladies, but I could see the elation on his face, the pure rush of having conquered one of his biggest fears.

"You handled that like a champ." I resisted the urge to hug him tighter and plant a huge kiss on his face. I could wait until we were home to embarrass him. "You want to grab ice cream when we're done here?"

"Yeah!" His eyes lit up. "Can Lily come?"

"If it's okay with Lily and her mom."

Anna's hands moved rapidly as she relayed the question to her daughter. "Lily, love, do you want to get ice cream with Daren after your swim?"

Lily's head bobbed up and down in an enthusiastic nod and began signing rapidly at Daren.

"That's a yes, if it wasn't obvious," her mom laughed. "She's asking Daren what his favorite ice cream flavor is."

"Peanut butter chocolate!" My son forgot all about being afraid and started an adorably clumsy swim toward his friend. "My sister's is strawberry shortcake, but she likes everything pink. Pink and llamas."

Anna hurriedly translated Daren's words before the kids started swimming off. "Ah well, they'll figure it out," she laughed. "She couldn't stop talking about making a friend on her first day of school. I was so worried about her adjusting to living here, so her finding Daren is a huge weight off my mind."

"I'm glad to see it too," I told her, propping my arms up on the ledge. "He's a quiet kid, usually keeps to himself, so it's nice to see him coming out of his shell. Especially for someone who needed a friend." We watched the kids quietly for another minute before I asked, "Where are you all from?"

"Illinois, originally. But we moved around a lot after the Collapse and came here from Jerriton."

"Ah, it's not too bad up there anymore, is it?" We were in regular contact with the folks running the Jerriton territory, many of them were the same people who pulled through for us against the Sha.

"Oh no, we loved it up there! Sadly, the schools were lacking, especially for Lily's needs. And my husband landed a great position at the hospital here, so it was a no-brainer."

"Oh, what's your husband do? He's probably met my wife."

"He's an EMT. He was actually a medic in the Jerriton army when they overthrew the last governor."

"No shit, Mari did the same! She was a nurse, then a war medic, and now she just became a gyne-cologist." I folded my arms and rested my head on them, smiling at the thought of her. "She wanted to deliver babies, and now she finally gets to. The whole crumbling of civilization just derailed things a bit."

"It was the same for Colby." Anna laughed lightly.

"We're ready for a quiet life. He just wants to drive an ambulance and hang out with the kiddo."

"Well, you guys came to the right place."

I looked over my shoulder to watch Daren, but he was absolutely fine. Lily seemed to be coaxing him to put his face in the water, even handing him her goggles so he could see. He pressed the lenses to his eyes and took a big breath before barely skimming the water with his face. When he looked up again, Lily clapped and encouraged him.

I already knew those two would be inseparable. Hopefully, we could talk Lily's parents into coming over so they could keep hanging out, and we could have new adults to talk to as well. Even though all of us were well known and respected in Four Corners, some of the other parents were still weirded out by four of us being married to one woman.

Logically, I could understand it—I was the same way years ago. It didn't make the judgments and assumptions any less annoying. But all that mattered was that our kids were safe. We, their *five* parents, just needed to keep providing a stable environment for them and continue being blissfully happy with our dynamic—which worked out great for childcare, by the way.

Anna and her husband would figure it out eventually and make that judgment call themselves. If they didn't want to hang out with us, it was their loss. We threw the best parties in town.

I only hoped, if they did feel that way, they wouldn't keep Lily from seeing Daren. Sending my friends away was one of my dad's favorite ways to be an asshole when I was a kid. So far, I was pretty good at doing the opposite of everything my old man did, and I had no intention of breaking that streak.

"Hey, Daren!"

My son looked up. He'd gotten as far as sticking his nose and mouth in the water and blowing bubbles. I didn't expect to see that for another six months.

I tapped a finger on my wrist, not that I had a watch on. "Fifteen more minutes, then we're getting ice cream."

"Yes! You're the best, Dad!"

I smiled and looked down at my left hand where I wore a gunmetal wedding band. Reaper's mom made them years ago for all of us guys. "I'm definitely in the top four, but I'll take it."

MARIPOSA

Standing in front of the bathroom mirror, I unwound the towel from my head and used it to scrub through my damp hair. Once my hair was dry enough, I started brushing.

The house was blissfully quiet, a rarity these days. Reaper, Jandro, and Gunner were playing some elaborate game in the backyard with the kids. They made cardboard swords and armor and planned several epic battles and sieges across the yard. Last I heard, Daren was a prince saving a village of innocent chicken-people from the dangerous giants who wanted to eat them.

In any case, it was a great way to keep them busy while Doctor Mommy got some time to herself. I had just finished my bath and planned to grab a glass of wine before joining the others out back.

I finished brushing my hair and started putting on

my lotion when I heard the front door open. Shadow's soft, "Hey, Freyja," floating up brought a smile to my lips. He walked through the house, likely checking out the epic battle in the backyard before coming to find me.

"I'm in here, love," I called when his footsteps ascended the stairs.

Shadow appeared in the doorway a moment later, his lips parting and eyes taking me in appreciatively. "Hey, lover. Do you...want some help?"

I smiled coyly at him in the mirror, both of us knowing exactly where his "help" would lead. "From you, always."

He walked up behind me and picked up the lotion bottle from the counter. It was only as he poured a small amount into his palm and rubbed his hands together that I noticed the tension in his shoulder. There was some stiffness, even an undercurrent of aggression in his movements and how tightly his brow furrowed.

"How was your tattoo appointment?" I ventured.

Shadow let out a non-committal grunt, placing his hands on my back to rub the lotion in.

"Bad client?" I tried again.

"The worst," he admitted. "Changed his mind about the design constantly, made scheduling a night-mare, and he's always coming up short on his deposits with tons of excuses. I'm thinking about dropping him."

"Then you should." I leaned my head back until it rested on his chest. "There are tons of people who would love to be a client of yours. Give his spot to someone who would appreciate you."

"I know, you're right. It's so fucking frustrating because in the moment, he tries to make *me* seem like the unreasonable one."

"Well, he's full of shit." Shadow was rubbing lotion into my shoulders and I reached up to grab his hands. "Even if you were unreasonable, which you're not, it's *your* fucking business. Run it however you want to."

Shadow's lips curled into a smile as he gradually relaxed. "I thought about playing dumb and fucking up his design even more so he'd finally go somewhere else."

"That's an idea." I laughed. "Draw him a pile of dogshit, because that's exactly how he's acting."

"Tempting." Shadow kissed my cheekbone before grabbing for the lotion bottle again. "Thanks for letting me vent, lover."

"Always." I angled my head, reaching on tiptoes to kiss the corner of his jaw. "I'm sorry you had a rough day."

"It's fine." He was lotioning my lower back now, large hands spanning around to my waist. "I just need to decompress from the day."

"Is this helping?" I reached up to touch more of him, my fingers grazing his neck and shoulders.

"Very much," he purred. His hands roamed over my belly and lower ribs, firm and steadfast in his task despite me being completely naked.

When he reached for more lotion, I arched against him, stretching my body long as I reached up and pressed my chest forward. My hands massaged into his neck while my bare ass pressed into the front of his jeans.

"Hold still," he commanded. "I need to get all of you."

I brought my hands to the counter with a small pout. It turned into a breathy gasp when Shadow's lotion-slicked hands came to my ass. He kneaded and massaged each side with a firm thoroughness that wasn't entirely sexually motivated. When he set his mind to a task, he wanted to see it through, whether that was tattooing, doing a project with the kids, or covering his wife from head to toe with lotion.

My fingers curled on the bathroom counter while I fought the urge to press and wiggle for more of his thorough touch. I bit back a moan as Shadow went for more lotion and then knelt behind me.

His rubdown began on my left thigh, just under my ass. My knees felt weak at the first touch, at the pressure of his thumbs running up and down the back of my leg before circling around to the front of my thigh. He was just as thorough on my calf and shin, never missing an inch. By the time he reached my foot and ankle, my heartbeat was pounding harder between my legs than in my chest.

"Lift up your foot, lover." Shadow's breath blew warm air on my hip when he spoke the gentle command.

I did as he said, then my hands curled into fists as he pressed into the arch. His large hands massaged my foot with such care, even getting lotion between my toes and rubbing deeply into my heel.

When Shadow placed my foot back on the floor, it was more than enough for me. "Get up, I want you."

"I have to do your other leg." His tone was full of mirth as he reached for the lotion again but grew rougher when I started to turn around. "Stay where you are. I'm not done."

Growling out my frustration, I slapped my hands on the counter and faced the mirror. My skin was already flushed with the branding heat of his touch, but it wasn't enough. I wanted to *see* red marks from his hands, his mouth. I already ached for his thick cock to spread me apart.

"Better not take too long," I warned him as he diligently massaged lotion into my right leg. "The kids could come back inside any minute."

"They won't," he said confidently. "They're very busy protecting the chicken coop."

I heard a loud crack that echoed throughout the tiled bathroom and then a moment later, heat and stinging pain bloomed over my ass cheek.

"That's for trying to rush me," Shadow said, amusement filling his voice. "Now give me your foot."

The combined sensations of his thorough, gentle care of lotioning my foot and the echoing pain of my ass were a heady mixture. I loved his sweetness and affection and craved his rougher handling. He needed some control right now, so I wouldn't push him too much. I would be good and patient and let him finish his task as he wanted, no matter how tempting it was to just sit on his face.

Shadow stood once he finished my legs, and I swallowed my whine when he reached for the lotion bottle again. I was completely covered at this point. What more did he need to do?

The answer came when he reached forward and grabbed my breasts, lotion-covered palms rolling slickly over the sensitive skin.

"Is this how you wanted me to touch you?" His mouth hovered near my ear, voice lowered to a tantalizing whisper. "To get you so ready and wet for me?"

"Yes," I squeaked on a ragged breath, fighting to keep still as he ordered me.

Shadow's mouth dropped, sucking a hard kiss on the crook of my neck as he squeezed my tender nipples between his fingers. "But you're already wet for me, aren't you?"

"Check and see," I challenged him. *So much for being good.*

Shadow's hands fell to my waist, where he spun

me away from the counter to face the bedroom. He did it so quickly, I was barely aware it happened until he swatted me on the ass.

"Get on the bed. Hands and knees."

I hurried to obey. Shadow was never dominant in an angry or mean way, but he was a relentless tease when I became too bratty.

"Scoot back towards me, to the very edge of the bed. Legs wider. Yes, there."

I stopped in the exact position and place he wanted me, the only sound being my ragged breaths of anticipation. If I looked back at him, I knew he'd keep denying me. So I faced forward, looking at the far bedroom door while the tension mounted higher with every passing second.

Shadow touched my lower back after what felt like an eternity, smoothing a palm up my spine before running it lower to the tender flesh of my ass.

"Beautiful," he let out softly before dropping his hand.

I pulled my lip between my teeth, fighting the urge to cry out and beg. He was so close but didn't touch me directly. I *craved* him, goddamnit. Couldn't he see how ready and wet I was?

A soft thud came from behind me, almost making me turn to look. The next thing I felt was Shadow's arms looping through my legs to hold my waist from underneath. The motion pulled my hips back directly onto his waiting mouth.

"Ohh, Shadow..." I whimpered at the pressure and friction of his lips on me, his beard rough on my sensitive flesh.

He moaned out some wordless answer, vibrations thrumming through my pussy as he ate me. His tongue and lips moved constantly, sucking and licking at me like an indulgent meal. I tried to squirm, but he held me in place with a firm grip. One hand slid low down my belly until he cradled my clit between two fingers, but he wouldn't let me rock or squirm to get more friction there. Only his mouth devouring me and his powerful grip directed where I moved.

"Shadow…" I was shaking from the intensity swarming over me from the relentless pleasure running through my system faster than I could breathe.

He let out a long "Mmmm," in reply, and only then loosened his hold enough to let me rock against his face and hands. It was the smallest tilting of my hips that he allowed, but it was enough. It allowed me to grind my clit into his firm fingers, a sigh escaping me at the much-needed pressure.

My rocking motions must have done favorable things to my ass, because his face pulled away and he slapped and grabbed at my flesh with hungry growls. I felt the sharp bite of teeth on my left cheek and gasped, only to hear his soft rumble of laughter and then a light caress and kiss to soothe the pain away.

"What do you want, lover?" Shadow's mouth was

so close to my needy pussy, I could still feel the vibrations of his voice and shivered.

"I want you," I whined, still grinding into his solid fingers against my clit. "I need you."

A soft hum of approval left his mouth and then the pressure of a long, tongue-filled kiss between my legs nearly had me full-on collapsing down to the bed.

"You're so close. So beautiful." He was practically whispering to himself, taking long licks, sucks, and kisses of me between each statement. "Delicious. So perfect."

"Shadow," I pleaded, near tears. My fingers curled painfully around the bed sheet, every muscle so wound up and tight and desperate for release.

"Make yourself come. I'm not stopping you."

Oh, that smug bastard. If I could move any more, I'd back up and smother him in this pussy he liked to eat so much.

"I need more," I begged. "I need you to…to…"

"Yes?" He prompted with another playful bite on my ass cheek. "What do you need?"

"I need you to fuck me."

"Before you come? Absolutely not."

A frustrated groan dragged out of my chest and I brought my face and chest down to the bed, my arms already too fatigued to stay upright from all this work.

Shadow chuckled, shifting his hold around me to smooth a hand up my spine. Kisses rained down on my lower back, but I was paying attention to his other hand delving between my legs.

"My beautiful wife," Shadow purred, the weight of his entire hand massaging my clit in earnest now. "You've given me everything."

He really took it seriously when I said a woman's mind was the key to her pleasure. Every word hit me with such emotional intensity that translated instantly to more pleasure in my body. Especially because I knew how much he meant it.

My orgasm swept over me like a tidal wave, amplified by the pleased groan from Shadow as he watched me. His sure, confident hand carried me through the crest and the fall. The kisses and whispered praise on my skin were the cherries on top.

His hand fell away while I sucked in ragged breaths of air, my pulse thick and thrumming in every sensitive point. Then his warm hand returned to my back, and his silky, blunt head spread apart my tender flesh.

"Yes." My spine bowed into a deep arch, hips pressing back to receive him. I looked over my shoulder to see that he'd gotten completely undressed. "Fuck, you're so hot."

The early afternoon light brought a soft, even quality to his skin. No harsh shadows to accentuate his scars or the carved depth of his muscles. He still looked huge and powerfully built, but seeing him in daylight like this illustrated who he was. He hadn't been an assassin, a killer in the shadows, for years. He was my husband and a devoted dad who cherished his family.

Shadow looked up from where we joined, smiling shyly at my astute observation, but there was a roguish smirk in that handsome face too. "You are," he retorted, a blush creeping up his neck.

He pressed forward slowly, making short thrusts to coat himself with my wetness and acclimate me to his size. Even just that had me breathless and babbling, he was so *thick*. So kind and loving, with just enough dominance to make me want to quiver and melt.

Another wave of emotion had me pressing up to kneeling, leaning back until my head touched his shoulder and my back grazed his chest. Immediately, I was taken back to that service center where I'd traveled across the continent to find him. We'd been in a position much like this after he'd accepted that I'd love him no matter what and agreed to return home with me.

Shadow immediately cupped my face with a gentle hand, bringing my gaze to his. "You okay, lover?"

"Yes." I stroked my fingers through his beard, all the joy and elation of having this man's love swirling madly in my chest. "I just love you, that's all."

"I love you." He kissed me so tenderly, thumb stroking over my cheekbone, that it kicked up the swarm of emotions in my chest like a hornet's nest.

We stayed like that, kissing and touching each other's faces like our very first time. I didn't even realize a small happy tear had leaked out of my eye until Shadow wiped it away. "Do you want to keep going?" he asked softly. "Or stop?"

I absolutely wanted to keep going, but I heard the backyard slider open and close before I could answer. Footsteps started clamoring up the stairs, too heavy to be either of the kids, but I still grabbed for the bed sheet to cover up.

Shadow and I froze at the sight of Reaper, pausing wide-eyed in the bedroom doorway before a slow, knowing smile pulled across his face. "Am I interrupting anything?"

"No, but," I clutched the sheet to my chest, "are the kids coming inside?"

"Not yet." Reaper wiped his brow, biting back a wider smile. "I've been attacking Chicken Village for the past hour and was gonna grab a quick shower."

He didn't move from the doorway, the unspoken question hanging in the air. Shadow and I quickly glanced at each other, the two of us grinning impishly. Still, Reaper was considerate enough not to be presumptuous.

"I'll just shower downstairs if you want to—"

"Don't be ridiculous," Shadow barked. "Join us."

MARIPOSA

Once he got the clear invitation, Reaper wasted no time. He kicked off his boots and tore out of the rest of his clothing with a speed that was almost comical. One of these days, I'd have to make the guys do nice, slow stripteases for me.

"You smell sweet, sugar. Did you just have a bath?" Reaper walked on his knees across the bed, and I leaned away from Shadow to greet him with a kiss.

"Yes, and Shadow was nice enough to lotion me up."

Reaper clicked his tongue. "Such a shame to dirty you up again."

"A tragedy," Shadow mused, returning his hands to my hips to press deeper inside me with a small thrust. He'd stayed hard and inside me the whole time we'd been kissing, and now my body stretched deliciously to receive more of him.

Reaper held my face and kissed me in a similar way, but with his signature roughness that sent wild thrills down my spine. He conquered my mouth, tongue pressing inside and lips scraping against mine. The weight of his hand kept me still as Shadow began a slow rocking motion of his hips.

I moaned into Reaper's mouth, relishing in the feeling of being trapped between them. Reaper scooted closer, bringing a deep arch to my back as his punishing kiss never relented. I groped up his thighs, feeling my way to his cock, only to have my hand batted away.

Reaper chuckled at my whine, his grip sliding to my throat as he broke the kiss with an evil smile.

"You get me in your pussy and nowhere else today," he said. "Once Shadow gets you nice and slick for me."

I whimpered through Shadow's thrusts dragging through me with increasing intensity, the way he stretched and filled me taking my breath away to desperate gasps. Reaper's hand on my throat was light enough for me to breathe, but I still couldn't beg and whine at him like I wanted to.

"Want to touch you," I whispered, skimming my fingertips up his leg once more, only to be denied again.

"I know." Reaper dropped another harsh kiss to

my mouth, catching my lip in his teeth as he pulled away. "But I want to fuck you hard and make you come on my cock until you fucking can't anymore."

Shadow let out a groan behind me, the force of his hips snapping harder against my ass. He released my waist with one hand to crack his palm against my left cheek, the fire and sting making me cry out.

"Fuck, look at what you're doing to me." Reaper released my throat to grab my hair, angling my head down to see his erection swinging stiffly between our bodies, woefully untouched.

"Can I just taste you a little?" My voice was barely audible over the crashing of Shadow's thrusts against my ass, but Reaper heard me just fine.

He yanked my head back, fist tightening in my hair as he grazed that cocksure smile against my lips. "Taste me all you want, sugar."

I groaned out my frustration but opened my mouth to accept the kiss anyway. If I couldn't suck him, my tongue on his was better than nothing.

I never knew when these games would crop up with him, always just as torturous as they were fun. He never did this when we were alone together. When it was just us, sex was an indulgent, full-body experience, and he held nothing back.

While with the others, he liked to play. Sometimes he controlled the scene, deciding what I would be allowed or denied, but always with the intent of heightening my pleasure in the end.

It was a healthy outlet for him, I realized. The club was no longer as active as it once was, and Reaper had come a long way since loosening up on his controlling tendencies. But the bedroom was where I craved his control and where he excelled at it.

"Fuck," Shadow growled out. His thrusts grew hurried, desperate. He crashed into me at full force, using me to chase his pleasure that was just out of reach. The drag of his heavy cock through me hit every nerve ending and made me squirm in Reaper's steel grip.

"Oh, look at you, loving getting fucked so much." Reaper placed both hands on me now, one in my hair and the other on my throat. He held me still for Shadow to pound into me, the rough clap of our bodies echoing off the walls. At any point, the others could come inside and know exactly what was happening. And that heightened the thrill even more.

"I'm getting so close." Shadow's gruff voice hovered close to my ear, his forehead touching near Reaper's hand on the back of my head. "Fuck, it's just too good."

"Touch her. Make her come before I take her," Reaper ordered. His grip tightened along the pulse points in my neck, lips hovering over mine in a kiss just out of my reach. "Do you love Shadow's cock splitting you apart, sugar?"

"Yes," I choked out in a strangled whisper. Shadow's hand found my clit at Reaper's command and strummed me with practiced expertise. My body wound up tight like a bowstring between them, unable to move or ease how they tormented me from either end. All I could do was feel and take.

I whined louder, desperate and needy as Shadow's fingers walked me toward another orgasm. His cock swelled inside me and amplified that need. The sting of Reaper's grip in my hair and his pressure on my throat swept me up in a perfect, raging storm of pleasure that was nearly painful.

My orgasm hit me like a bolt of lightning, spreading through my nerves like an all-consuming wildfire. Fingers curled into the flesh of my hips and heat flooded my core. Shadow moaned out his orgasm, the sound deep and animal-like over the blood pounding in my ears.

Pressure released on my neck and the room spun, the pulses of my orgasm suddenly squeezing around nothing. Then just as quickly, a thick cock pressed into me, driving deep and taking me with long, aggressive thrusts with no preamble.

Reaper, I realized in the dizzying haze of my orgasm. He was behind me now, looking down at where he was fucking me like he promised he would. His arms were tight and corded from where he gripped me roughly. His abs flexed with each rough thrust against my ass, and his breaths dragged raggedly out of his chest.

He barely gave me any chance to recover, and I

felt another orgasm building. My frayed nerve endings had no choice but to respond to the rough, delicious assault of him.

A caress on my cheek brought my attention forward. Shadow. He kneeled on the bed in front of me, his softening cock glossy with my wetness. I rested my head against his hip, so weak and wobbly as Reaper fucked me into oblivion.

"That's it. Lean on me, lover," Shadow purred with a gentle stroke over my hair. "Is it too much?"

Reaper slowed his thrusts just a fraction at the question, waiting for my response. He'd make it intense, maybe even painful. But he'd never give me more than I could handle.

"No...no, it's just...ohh, fuck!"

Another orgasm rippled out of me, much to Reaper's delight. He swatted my ass, grunted out some curses, and kept up his brutal pace. He over-loaded my senses in the best ways, and I found myself grabbing and clawing at Shadow through my release.

"Yes, use me, lover." Shadow stroked my neck with light, reverent touches. The one thing he would never do was grab my throat. "Scratch me, bite me. Take what you need to let it out."

Reaper drove into me even harder at that, as if taking the offer as a challenge. I looked at him over my shoulder while clinging to Shadow's waist like a lifeline. Reaper smirked back at me before lifting a hand to smack down on my ass again. He wanted to drive me into a frenzy of orgasms and practically maul Shadow in the process.

And I was helpless to do anything but take it, holding on to Shadow with nails and teeth while I came apart.

My pleasure rose and fell in intensity, but it never felt like each orgasm actually began and ended. They rolled into each other like waves crashing on a beach as Reaper crashed into me. I groaned, gasped, and screamed, clawing at the solid wall of Shadow and making his skin bright red. He hissed and grunted but loved the pain, especially when I was rough with him during an orgasm. I could never hurt him seriously, so I didn't hold back as another bolt of pleasure stabbed through my clit like lightning. My mouth latched onto his hip bone, teeth clamping down as his body muffled my scream.

"Oh fuck, I love it when you come this hard." Shadow's grip was loose in my hair, just keeping the strands out of my face.

"Can't take much more," I panted, leaning my forehead on his lower stomach.

"Oh, you've got at least one more in you," Reaper taunted, his breath tight. He was rock-solid and expanding inside me, his forceful rhythm stuttering as he neared his limit.

Shadow stroked down my side, his fingers grazing the edge of my breast, and I shivered at the contact.

"She's really sensitive everywhere." Shadow

sounded pleased, continuing a featherlight touch down to my waist and across my back. "So fucking beautiful."

"Keep touching her like that." Reaper's voice was bright with a new idea, his rough thrusts slowing down to deep, languid strokes.

My body was abuzz with the change in sensations, the gentle strokes almost more intense than the spanks and hard fucking. Shadow's touch continued up my back, bringing on another body-wracking shiver when he reached the nape of my neck. He then dragged his fingers down on either side, reaching underneath me for my nipples.

I cried out when he rolled them between his fingers, the peaks so taut and sensitive it was nearly painful. "No, don't stop," I begged when he paused.

Shadow's pleased rumble vibrated over me, eliciting another shiver, like he'd touched me with another limb. "Can you come for us one more time, lover?"

"I…I think…" I was in some hazy place between feeling numb and overly sensitive. My heartbeat wouldn't slow down, and I was exhausted.

Shadow pinched down harder. At the same time, Reaper delivered a smack to the other side of my ass on unmarked skin. The sharp sensations at both points brought my focus back, gave me something new to chase amidst the constant buzz in my body.

"Oh, fuck yeah, that's it." Reaper's thrusts stopped

altogether as I rocked back and forth on his length, using him to ride the high I needed. "Fuck me, sugar."

"Spank me again," I begged.

He did so, rubbing the tender flesh in between each hard smack of his palm. My orgasm was finally building, growing like a fire as I kept pressing back and riding him desperately. Shadow kept my nipples clasped between his fingers, holding firm and steady as I came apart.

I lost count of how many times Reaper spanked my ass, but when I finally shattered, he was there with me. I sank into the mattress, well and truly spent by the shockwaves rolling over me. Reaper grabbed my hips for his final surge forward, shuddering and cursing as he spilled his release. His hands slapped to the bed on either side of me, keeping himself from collapsing onto my back.

"Still want a shower?" I asked once I had enough breath in my lungs.

He huffed out a laugh, lowering to ghost kisses along my back. "Take one with me."

I looked up at Shadow. "Sorry, you might have to rub me down again."

"Oh no." He grinned and swept hair out of my face. "What a shame."

EIGHT

SHADOW

I jolted upright in bed, my heart beating mercilessly at my sternum and my skin covered in a cold sweat.

Shit, that was a bad one. The worst I've had in a while.

I sought to ground myself and catch my breath while the nightmare ebbed away. The room was dark, but I saw Mari clearly, wrapped up in one of the others as they slept. I tipped my head back and found the headboard of our bed, curled my fingers to feel the sheets underneath me.

I'm home. I'm okay.

My throat was as parched as a bone, and I itched for some light and open space. Just to calm my senses so I could go back to sleep.

I swung my feet to the floor and found a pair of sweatpants to put on, then moved silently out of our bedroom and down the stairs. Once in the kitchen, I flicked on the light and filled a big glass of water from the tap. I drank it and filled it three times before pausing to take a breath.

Bracing my hands on the edge of the sink, I stepped back and tried to assess the sudden nightmare without spiraling into anxiety.

Had I been stressed lately? No, not really. My one shitty client was gone. The tattoo shop was always busy, but I'd been able to hand more work off to my apprentice. The kids seemed happy with school and all of their activities. Rori had her tantrums, but that was normal. Everything between Mari, me, and the guys was fine.

Was it the anniversary of something? Going to prison, getting out of prison, getting captured by the Sha, or confronting my mother's ghost?

I couldn't find something concrete to pinpoint as the reason for my first nightmare in almost a year. Dr. Ellis said they would show up randomly sometimes, but there was usually some underlying cause.

"Daddy?"

I whipped around to see a sleepy, bedheaded Rori blinking at me just outside of the kitchen. She had on her favorite llama-print pajama set and was already outgrowing it, hands and feet sticking far out of the sleeves.

"Hey, sweetheart." I straightened, stepping away from the sink. "What are you doing up?"

"Um." She rubbed her eyes and avoided the question, which meant she was probably reading picture books or playing after we said lights out. "Did the monsters try to get you, Daddy?"

I smiled at her. Gunner scared the kids with stories of monsters under the bed on Halloween, but she had no idea how real monsters could be.

"They tried but they couldn't get me." I lowered to a crouch, holding my arm out to her. "Come here."

Rori shuffled over and leaned heavily on me from how tired she was. I groaned as I lifted her up, holding her against my side as I came to standing.

When did I become a dad to five-year-olds? It seemed like we had just brought the twins home from the hospital. Rori and her brother used to be shorter than my forearm, their heads fitting comfortably in my palm with room to spare. I refused to carry them upstairs for weeks, terrified that I'd drop one of our infants.

Now my daughter was a hefty weight on my hip, her legs dangling past my waist, and squirmier than Freyja when she didn't want to be held anymore.

I tickled one of Rori's feet as I turned back to the kitchen, earning a few giggles and light kicks on my ribs. "Do you want some milk, Ror-meister?"

She nodded, settling down with her head on my shoulder. *Lechita, por favor.*

"Very good." I kissed her forehead, pleasantly surprised. "You'll have to tell Papi Jandro the new words you know."

I opened the fridge, grabbed the milk and her sippy cup, poured the milk and put the lid on, all using my left hand. I thought being ambidextrous came in handy as an assassin, but I found it much more useful in parenting.

"Careful now." I handed Rori her drink. "Don't spill."

Rori took her cup in both hands, and I refilled my water from the sink before heading to the couch to sit. We were *mostly* quiet for a few moments, the only sound being Rory's noisy drinking as she nestled into my side.

"Daddy?" she piped up.

"Yes, my dearest daughter." I curled one finger through a lock of her hair.

"Did the monster give you all your owies too?"

I froze. My mind came to a screeching halt, body tensing up so abruptly that Rori noticed it immediately. She shifted around, wearing a puzzled expression as she tried to get a better look at my face.

I knew our kids were smart, perceptive. But, fuck me, I was not ready to talk about this. When it came to the kids, I didn't know if I ever would be. I had been younger than them when the Sisterhood first started cutting me.

Becoming a dad for the first time, and seeing first-hand how fragile and innocent children were, made me want them to never experience even a mere sliver of the suffering I had endured.

Rori once fell from a play structure and cut her chin on the pavement. There was so much blood, and I panicked. I rushed her directly to Mari at the hospital, where I proceeded to spiral and freak out some more. I told Mari I couldn't do it. I couldn't be a father, I let my child *get hurt*. Rori had screamed and cried bloody murder the whole way over because I failed to protect her.

Mari then calmly explained that it wasn't my fault. Kids fell all the time and sometimes got hurt. It was normal. Their bodies were constantly growing, and it was how they learned their limits. Rori was fine after a few small stitches and a lollipop. As fragile as they were, children were also resilient.

I should have known. Somehow I survived to adulthood, after all.

While I learned to be less extreme in my reactions, it didn't make answering my daughter's question any easier. I brushed my fingers through Rori's hair, still trying to find the right words.

"No monster is ever going to hurt you." A flash of anger burned through me and I found myself growling. If that fucking cult got within a mile of my children, no force on earth or among the gods would stop me from annihilating them.

"Sometimes monsters look like nice people," I went on. "Sometimes they'll pretend to be your friend. So if anyone makes you sad or scared, or they just give you a weird feeling in your tummy," I poked

Rori's belly for effect, "you don't have to be friends with them, okay? That goes for now and when you're a grown-up. Anyone at all who makes you feel bad."

"Okay, Dad," she said quietly, her eyelids drooping.

I huffed out a soft laugh and leaned down to plant a kiss in her hair. "Finish your milk, then let's go back to bed."

Once she drained her cup, I returned our dishes to the kitchen and went to tuck her in.

"Your dads will protect you from monsters," I said, bringing her blanket under her chin. "Your mom too, she's fought plenty of them. You can always come to us, Ror-meister."

Rori's eyes blinked heavily, moments away from sleep. "Daren said he would watch over me too."

"Yeah, your brother is going to be big and strong one day. Just like your dads, huh?" I kissed her forehead and started to get up from her bedside.

"No...I mean, uncle Daren..."

My heart jumped into my throat as I stared down at her, stunned. "What did you say?"

But Rori had already fallen asleep.

NINE

REAPER

"There's the trailhead." Jandro pointed through the windshield.

"'Kay. Let me find a place to park."

"Bro, you can stop literally anywhere. There's no one around." Jandro turned in the passenger seat to grin at the kids behind us. "We've got the canyon to ourselves, guys! Are you excited?"

"Yes! Can I get out?" Rori kicked in her carseat, fumbling at her seatbelt.

"Rori, no," I told her. "Wait 'til I stop the car, you know the rules."

She stilled with a pout while Daren made signs with his hands.

"English or Spanish, son. I'm happy you're learning ASL, but we don't know what you're saying," Jandro said.

"I said, I hope we see a coyote."

Daren's hands moved swiftly as he connected the words. Every day he grew more confident with signing, and he really seemed taken with it since meeting his new friend, Lily. Shadow had even been practicing with him a bit. The big guy seemed thrilled to find something they could bond over.

"No coyotes, probably." I glanced at Daren in the rearview mirror, still signing to himself. "They'll be sleeping now and wake up to hunt when it starts getting dark."

I pulled over at the mouth of the canyon, finding a sliver of shade to park under. This place was one of the smaller canyons in the area. It didn't even have a name as far as I was aware, but it was pretty, scenic, and an easy hike. A perfect outing for a couple of squirrelly five-year-olds.

Mari, Shadow, and Gunner all had work or something else going on, so Jandro and I elected to take the kids out. It would be good for Hades too, who was currently seated between the two kids. His head was already swiveling from side-to-side, ever watchful for any threats to his tiny humans.

Hades, the god, hadn't spoken to me again since that night at the party eight years ago. But I wasn't entirely convinced he'd left this dog's body completely.

"Alright, we're here. Aurora May, don't run off," I warned, opening my door.

"I just want to seeee—"

"Come here, let me get your sunscreen and your

hat on so you don't burn. Do you need to use the bathroom?"

"No. Can I pick a flower for Mommy?"

"In a second, sugar cube."

Jandro got Daren situated while I handled Rori. Hades sniffed around our perimeter as we got the kids ready, then let out a soft bark of approval and sat when he was satisfied.

I put a dog treat in Rori's hand. "Go give that to Hades and we can start exploring."

"Papi, can I sit on your shoulders?" Daren asked Jandro. "I want a better view."

"Alright, just for a little bit." Jandro picked him up and seated him behind his neck, Daren's legs draping down over his chest. "You're gonna turn your old dad into a hunchback."

"You already are," I joked, following after Rori and Hades who had already ventured into the canyon. "Rori, stay close. Don't go off the trail."

"I know, *Dad*." Her tone was snotty, like she was already fifteen instead of five. *Ah, kids.*

"You remember what happened last time?" I couldn't resist teasing her.

"Yes, I remember!" She turned around and shot me a dirty look.

I made a similar face back at her until she laughed, then pulled her into a quick hug against my leg. "I love you, Ror. It's always an adventure with you."

On the last hike we went on, Rori went off the trail to get a closer look at a jackrabbit. She ended up walking over a young cactus plant, and Mari spent the better part of a night pulling the spines out of her feet.

The risk wasn't as high here, with the canyon being fairly narrow and mostly shaded. It felt much cooler as we started walking through, the sandstone walls curving as if shaped by water on either side of us. People liked coming here because of the paintings on the canyon walls, left by indigenous cultures thousands of years ago.

I studied the pale, faded paintings as I walked through. Naturally, I couldn't interpret them like a scholar could, but even my untrained eye could make out figures, animals, and symbols.

That circle hovering above all the figures had to be the sun or moon, clearly sacred to people who depended on the land to survive. It got me wondering if any of *our* gods had reached these people in some way, or some version of them. Did they personify the sun, death, love, and healing? Did a god of the Underworld choose someone to carry out their commands like Hades had with me?

"Look, it's Horus!" Daren pointed up at the thin stripe of sky above us where several birds with impressive wingspans soared with ease.

"Ah, not quite." Jandro peered up, squinting at the

sky. "Horus is a lot smaller. Those guys are big. I'm pretty sure they're turkey vultures."

"What's that?" Daren held on to Jandro's face as he leaned back to get an even better look at the sky.

"They're scavengers, so they look for food that's already dead." Jandro turned his head and took a playful bite of Daren's leg. When our son shrieked and shook out of his grasp, Jandro exaggerated a face of disgust. "Ugh, nope. This boy's still very much alive."

Darren cackled with laughter, the bright sound echoing off the canyon walls, until Jandro lifted him off his shoulders and set him on the ground. "Go walk with your sister, my neck needs a break."

Jandro and I walked together, keeping an eye on the twins and Hades a few feet ahead of us. Rori had already discarded her hat, and her golden curls bounced with every step.

"Does it feel real yet?" Jandro knew what I meant. I asked him all the time during moments like this.

"Oh yeah." He grinned at me, rubbing the back of his neck. "Right now, it sure does. But that," he nodded ahead to the kids carefully tracing one of the wall paintings with their fingers, talking softly to each other, "seeing them explore, learn, and thrive with *us* guiding them?" His hand dropped, eyes locked with wonder on our two children. "I still can't believe it sometimes."

I patted at my pockets, searching for the phone I

rarely turned on because it barely worked half the time. A few local engineers had gotten some cell towers working last year, although reliable phone calls were still a long way off. But the phone had a camera, which was the only way I really used the piece of shit.

"Aw, Mari will love that," Jandro breathed as I held the phone up.

The kids stood in a patch of sunlight, framed by bright orange poppy flowers on either side of them. Their backs were to us—Rori's hair aglow like a halo and Daren's dark and glossy like raven feathers. Their hands were stretched out in front them, still running over the ancient wall paintings with a quiet, almost reverent curiosity.

I snapped pictures of them until Hades blocked my view. Since he didn't tell me who to kill anymore, his new favorite pastime was getting into every photo of the kids he possibly could.

The kids moved on, walking through the canyon while Hades sniffed ahead and Jandro and I trailed after.

"How you sleeping lately?" Jandro lowered his voice so only I could hear him.

"Fine." My knee jerk, default answer.

"Just fine?"

I swallowed. After everything he and I had been through, and now that we were raising a family together, he deserved more than a dismissive answer. Old habits die hard. Even all these years later, I was still working on the whole opening-up-emotionally thing.

"Yeah, I mean pretty good for the most part. The nightmares don't come around that much anymore, once every few months or so."

"Your doctor says that's normal?"

"There is no normal, really. Everyone processes shit differently. But it's better than a couple times a week like it was however long ago."

"Yeah, that's true. I just wanted to check on you." He knocked his shoulder into mine. "In case you needed anything."

Always such a caretaker. It was why Jandro took to being a dad so naturally.

"I'm good, dude," I assured him. "Really. I can actually say that without any bullshit now."

"That's a first," he snorted, then shot me a good-natured smile. "I'm glad to hear it." The kids moved on, wandering deeper into the canyon with Hades while we followed a few paces behind them. "It's crazy how uneasy we feel about life being so much simpler, isn't it?" Jandro mused.

"Yeah. Like this is temporary and we're waiting for the other shoe to drop."

My fingers twitched at my side, the cigarette craving hitting me hard. It always did when I thought of our past life, all the stress and fear we were under. I never smoked around the kids, only indulging when they stayed with grandparents for a few days so we could have our adult time.

"Eight years is hardly temporary," Jandro retorted.

I rolled my eyes toward him. "Everything is temporary. I just hope this peaceful period lasts through their lifetimes." I nodded my head at the twins. "Or if it doesn't, I hope that whatever comes next doesn't touch them."

Jandro's eyes narrowed, his hand coming up next to his ear. "You hear that, Reap?"

"Yeah, yeah, it's the sound of me being a sap. You're hilarious, man, but that one's getting old."

"No, I'm serious. You don't hear that hissing?"

I paused, cocking my head to listen. There was a breeze through the canyon, plus the sounds of insects echoing and distorting through the canyon walls.

"It's just the wind, dude. I don't—"

Hades growled, low and full of warning. I hadn't heard him make that sound in years. Fast and silent as a shadow, he darted in front of the children who were none the wiser.

"Hades, move your big butt." Rori pushed on his flank to get him out of her way, but he remained stiff, blocking her path with the broad side of his body.

"Rori, stop."

She turned to look at me, dismay on her face. "But why? I want to keep walking."

"Hades senses danger, sweetie. Come back to us, both of you."

Daren grabbed her hand and started to pull her back when I heard it. Not a hissing sound like Jandro initially thought, but a rattling.

"Fuck. Guys, freeze! Don't move." Jandro and I both put our palms out. The kids stopped in place, their eyes widening in fear.

"Move up and get them behind us," I said under my breath.

"You got it, Pres." Jandro put on a smile, brightening his voice. "Hey, guys, it's okay. Just stay still and let your dads come to you. You're doing great."

The rattling grew louder as we approached. I spotted movement just beyond Hades' head and fuck, that snake looked big and close. If the dog hadn't jumped in front of the kids, they might have stepped right on it.

Hades was stiff as a board, hackles raised and low growl constant in his throat. The rattlesnake was giving a warning, and so was he—touch my tiny humans and you're a dead snake.

"Easy, Hades. That's a good boy." Jandro and I made our way closer slowly, careful not to make any sudden movements and provoke the snake to become any more aggressive.

"Dad, I'm scared." Rori's lip wobbled, her eyes darting around fearfully until Daren pulled her into a hug, placing her head on his shoulder so she wouldn't look at the snake.

"You're okay, *mijita*." Jandro forced calm into his

voice, but I could hear how tense he was. "Just hold on to your brother, he's got you."

We reached the kids in one more step, then with an exchanged look and a nod, directed them behind us. Air whooshed out of my lungs with relief. I didn't even realize how tense I'd been.

Jandro and I kept our eyes forward, and one hand reached behind us to make sure our children stayed near.

"Start walking backwards," I instructed. "Slow."

Once we were a good twenty feet or so away from the snake, all four of us were able to relax.

Jandro swept Rori up into his arms, her expression still shaken as he hugged her tightly and planted kisses on her face. "Hey, you did great." He smiled exuberantly at her. "You did exactly as we said, even though you were scared. You're so brave."

With relief filling my chest, I picked up Daren, who only made a small grunt of protest, but otherwise leaned into me and hugged around my neck.

"You're a hero, kid," I told him. "That was a great thing you did, making your sister look away. It kept her calm, which was exactly what we needed."

Daren shrugged like it was no big thing, but I saw his face brighten at being called a hero. "I just didn't want her to get more scared."

It floored me how much he was exactly like his namesake, my brother. When my siblings and I were kids, I was always the asshole who scared Noelle and did stuff to make her cry. She'd run to Daren, who hugged her until she was calm. Likewise, as we got older, and his seizures got worse, Noelle always took care of him.

"You did all that and more." I kissed my Daren's temple. "I love you, son."

"Love you, Dad," he muttered, promptly wiping at where I kissed him. "Can you put me down now?"

"Alright," I groaned, bending to set his feet on the ground.

I looked over at Jandro who was gently rocking a now very tired-looking Rori. He caught my eye and smirked in my direction. "Enough adventure for one day, you think?"

"I'd say so." I ruffled Daren's hair. "You want to go Tess and Drea's for a cupcake?"

"Cupcake!" That woke Rori right up.

"Just what we need, kids high on cupcakes," Jandro chuckled, heading toward the car. "Better call the dog back, I think he's still in a staring contest with that snake." "Go on ahead." I patted Daren's back to follow them, then re-entered the canyon with a long whistle. "Hades! Come on back, mutt." He was in a darker area of the canyon and harder to see at this distance with his black fur, but when his head turned at the sound of my voice, I swore I saw...

"Hades?" I squinted across the distance, the hairs on my arms standing straight up. It couldn't be, but I thought for a second those weren't dog eyes looking back at me. They looked almost human and eerily intelligent.

"Hades." I somehow broke out of my stupor and patted my thigh. "Come here, boy."

The dog broke eye contact as he trotted over to me, tongue lolling out and his posture finally relaxed. I lowered to a crouch, scratching his ears and neck as I searched those big, dark eyes for that intelligence again. But he was all dog now, happy and smiling.

"Thank you for protecting my children," I said, then waited, searching his face for any kind of non-doglike response.

My heart stopped when those eyes met mine again, the ancient wisdom in them unmistakable.

It is not yet their time.

Just as quickly as it happened, it passed. Hades' eyes returned to wide and puppylike as he leaned forward to lick my face.

TEN

JANDRO

"**A**urora May Wilder!" I pointed my wrench across the yard. "This is the last time I'm telling you. Leave those chickens alone."

My daughter put on a big show of stomping away from the chicken coop with a pout, arms crossed over her chest. But my dad-senses knew she'd be meandering back that way once she thought I wasn't looking.

I'd been telling her all afternoon to leave them be. Some new chicks had just hatched and she wanted to pet and hold them, but getting close to the coop aggravated our younger rooster, Trombone. He had already rushed at Rori a few times, crowing and flapping aggressively. If she kept pushing his buttons, she was going to get pecked or cut with a spur.

And after I'd already yelled at her fifty times to

92

stay away, maybe it was a lesson she needed to learn the hard way.

"Jesus, these kids," I muttered, returning my attention to the motorcycle parts strewn out in front of me.

At my side, Larkan laughed as he stacked a set of piston rings. "I take it she's not getting a llama for her birthday?"

"Not in a million years," I huffed. "She needs to grow up, get rich, and get *me* a llama for my birthday."

"You can't have just *one* llama," Larkan's eight-year-old, Carter, chimed in matter-of-factly. "They're herd animals, so you need at least three."

"Then it's definitely not happening." I set my wrench down and wiped my hands on a rag, pointedly ignoring Rori as I gazed across the yard.

Noelle and Reaper were talking over whiskeys near the edge of the deck. Beyond them was a play fort we'd built a couple years ago. It had a slide, a small rock-climbing wall, and two solid wooden ladders to get up to the main area. Daren and his youngest cousin, Larkan Jr., who we all called Larkie, were horsing around in the fort, playing pirates or some such.

Mari, Shadow, and Gunner had gone off to ride for the day, which likely meant they went to the hot spring for skinny dipping, threesomes, and a picnic. Lucky bastards.

Not that I didn't love spending time at home with

the kids and other family. Just with Rori testing my patience today, it would have been nice to have some extra backup. Rori didn't test her mother or Shadow like she did me.

"What about goats?" Larkan and Carter were still on the subject of adding animals to our little farm.

"Mari does want a couple of goats," I admitted. "She wants a regular supply of goat cheese, and to watch them headbutt us, I'm sure." I lowered my head and bumped it softly into Carter while making a *bahhh* sound.

"Have you seen those goats that fall over when they get scared?" My nephew started giggling uncontrollably.

"That does *not* sound like an evolutionary advantage," I remarked. It was funny to think about, though.

Larkan sat back, his eyes lighting up. "You should think about getting some ducks too. Duck eggs are great, man."

"Do not put more animal ideas into my children's heads, please." I shook my wrench at him. "You're lucky Mari isn't here to endorse your suggestions."

"Ah, just you wait. Pretty soon it'll be like," Larkan started drumming a beat on the table, his grin too smug and satisfied as he sang, "*Old McJandro had a farm, E-I-E-I-O.*"

"Shut your mouth." I waved my wrench more menacingly at him. "Before I smack you."

He knew it was an empty threat and carried on making the animal noises while Carter's laughter rang across the yard. Reaper and Noelle even looked our way to see what the ruckus was about just as a high-pitched scream hit my eardrums.

I looked in the direction the sound came from and couldn't stop the single peal of laughter before slapping a hand over my own mouth. Rori was running as fast as she could go, shock and terror on her face, with Trombone the rooster right on her heels.

She ran straight toward Reaper, who scooped her up and shooed the rooster away with his foot.

"Knew this was gonna happen," I groaned, getting up from the table and heading their way to assess the damage.

Rori sobbed on Reaper's shoulder and clung to his neck, her face bright red as he rocked and shushed her. He rubbed her back and glared at me over her shoulder, a look that Trombone put on his face often. Reaper hated that rooster, and I knew he'd tear into me once the kids were in bed.

"Hey *mijita*, let's see." I went to look at the red mark on her leg, which thankfully wasn't bleeding, and was promptly swatted away by a tiny hand.

"No!" Rori had twisted in Reaper's arms, mean-mugging me as hard as a five-year-old could, still crying and sniffling.

"*Mami*," I gentled my voice. "I'm trying to make sure you're okay."

"No!" she repeated. "You *laughed* at me!"

It felt like someone had rammed a Rori-sized fist through my chest. Fuck, she'd heard that? Seen it?

"Rori, I..." There was no excuse, and I wasn't about to lie, so my words trailed off, speechless.

She turned back around to cling tighter to Reaper, crying into his shoulder while he kept looking at me with that heavy stare.

"Shhh, you're okay, sugar cube." He finally broke his glare to kiss her and soothe her. "Let's get you inside and clean your owies. That rooster's not gonna hurt you again." He shot another pointed look at me before turning to enter the house.

I just stood looking after them, feeling stunned, defeated, and guilty. A pat on my shoulder roused me from my stupor, and it was Noelle at my side, giving me a sympathetic look.

"Don't feel so bad, papa." She patted my shoulder again. "She'll forgive you."

"Will she, though?" I scratched a hand over my head. "Fuck, I didn't even mean to laugh, I just..."

"Honestly, it was funny." Noelle lowered her voice to a conspiratory whisper. "Just, better to laugh in hindsight than right when it's happening. Even *she* will think it's funny one day."

"I doubt that," I groaned, pinching my nose bridge.

"Sure she will. Larkie tells people all the time

about how he missed the potty a couple years ago. He thinks it's hilarious."

"That's 'cause your *boys* are foul." I grinned down at her. "Rori is a lady."

Noelle shoved playfully at my shoulder. "Go apologize to your daughter."

Yeah, that was the least of what I needed to do. Trombone would probably need to find a new home after this too.

I went inside to find Rori sitting on the kitchen counter, sniffling quietly as Reaper cleaned the welts on her legs with rubbing alcohol.

"How bad is it?" I asked.

He gave me a short glance over his shoulder. "Not bad. She just got pecked a couple times." He gathered up the cotton pads and dumped them in the trash with more force than necessary. "But I want that rooster gone. Tonight."

"Yeah. Yeah, of course. I'll go around to the neighbors in a sec and see if they want him. If not, I'll take care of it." With a hard swallow I looked past him to Rori, who was calmer but still sniffling and red-faced. "Are you feeling better, *mijita?*"

She gave a small nod. "A little."

"Good, I'm glad. I never want to see you scared or hurt." I edged closer to her, still giving her plenty of space. "I'm sorry I laughed, that was wrong. Sometimes even dads mess up and do the wrong thing."

She sniffed again. "I'm still mad at you."

"That's okay. I'm mad at me too. I wish I didn't do that." My hands flexed at my sides, wishing to give my daughter a hug, but it was more important right then to respect her space. "And it's not gonna happen again."

Just as my luck would have it, the rumble of bikes coming up the driveway announced Mari and the others coming home. Great, now I'd have to explain all this to *Shadow*, who Rori had thoroughly wrapped around her finger.

Predictably, she started sniffling louder once the door opened and her other parents spilled into the house. Mari and Gunner had their arms and fingers linked, laughing about something together. Shadow took one look at Rori and slid past them, his face hardening.

Aw, hell.

"What happened?" he demanded.

Rori hopped off the counter and ran to him, letting him scoop her up with one powerful arm and hold her protectively against his chest. That got Mari and Gunner's attention, untangling from each other and frowning at our girl's red, tear-soaked face.

"Oh sweetheart, are you okay?" Mari cooed, stroking her hair out of her eyes.

"Trombone bit me," Rori mumbled.

Shadow's gaze hit me like a cannonball to the chest, and I brought my hands up defensively. "We were all outside! I'd been telling her not to go near him all day."

"And Papi laughed at me," Rori went on.

"You *what?!*" Shadow looked more ready to murder me in that moment than during any of his sleepwalking episodes. If he wasn't holding Rori, I'm sure he would have decked me.

"Okay, let's all calm down." Mari put a hand on Shadow's shoulder and held her other arm out to Rori. "Want to wrap up in your llama blanket and relax? We can read a story."

Our daughter nodded slowly and allowed Shadow to pass her over. Once Mari took hold of her, she carried Rori toward her bedroom and shot us a look that said, *Figure this out amongst yourselves.*

"Did you seriously—" Shadow started at me again once they were gone, but Reaper stepped between us with his hand raised.

"Look, she's not badly hurt, which is the important thing. But she was really scared for a moment and that reaction," he gave me a disapproving look, "probably didn't make her feel any safer."

"I know, I know. I fucked up." My hand came to my forehead, rubbing where a headache started to build. "That's probably what's hurting her most and, believe me, I'm gutted to have done that. I'll make it up to her."

"You better," Shadow snarled.

"Probably gonna have to get her that llama after all," Gunner chimed in oh-so-helpfully.

"Great," I grumbled. "Fucking great."

"Seriously, though. She's been provoking the chickens despite you telling her not to, right?" Gunner came forward and clapped a supportive hand on my shoulder. "Now she knows the consequences, and she'll listen better next time."

"I guess, if she doesn't fucking hate me forever."

"She won't, man. And let's be honest." He brought his thumb and forefinger close together. "It was probably a *little* bit funny, right?"

"What the fuck are you saying?" Shadow growled. "Her being scared isn't funny."

Gunner whirled around to face him. "Dude, you laughed your ass off when that same rooster chased Mari all throughout the house when he got inside!"

Shadow leveled him with an incredulous look. "Yes, *Mari*. Who can handle one dumb fucking rooster. Rori is *five*."

"If she was in any *real* danger, of course I wouldn't have laughed, bro," I told him. "I'd put myself between her and whatever the threat was, like any of us would. But yeah, like Gunner said, she kind of had this coming."

"Sure, she did," Reaper cut in. "But laughing was the wrong response at the wrong time."

"I'll own up to that, definitely," I said. "And I'm getting rid of the rooster, so she doesn't continue to be afraid of him," I added with a sigh. "He's a nuisance, anyway. Foghorn's so chilled out now that he's an old man."

"I hate both of those birds, but Foghorn is easily my favorite of the two." Reaper opened a cabinet in search of more whiskey, the matter apparently settled. "If one of the new chicks happens to be male, maybe it'll bond with Rori and not act like a shithead towards her."

"Yeah, that's true." I gestured at the drinks he began pouring, beyond ready for one myself. "*Dámelo.*"

"Speaking of." Gunner nudged Shadow with a chuckle. "Did you know Trombone took a shit in Mari's hair that one time?"

Shadow, who had been in the middle of taking a drink, coughed and wheezed as he doubled over the counter. "No fucking way."

"I'm serious, I had to help her wash it out. Our battle-medic wife, who's seen buckets of blood and guts and shit, was like, *retching* because of a little rooster shit in her hair."

"Poor thing." Shadow's lip twitched in amusement.

"She was so grossed out, it was hilarious." Gunner raised his index finger in the air. "But my point is, that bird is a literal shithead, and he's better off on a dinner plate."

"Not saying I disagree, but I'm going to see if

anyone wants him alive first." I set my empty whiskey glass down and slid it across the counter to Reaper. "Linda down the street mentioned wanting a rooster, so I'll head over there now."

"What's wrong with her husband's cock?" Gunner's face lit up with the question like he'd been waiting for the perfect time to say it.

"Jesus, shut up," Reaper grumbled.

"Aw fuck off, you're no fun." Gunner turned away, looking out to the yard. "What are the boys playing?"

"Pirates, last I checked."

"Ooh, I want to be the sea monster!"

"Not the pretty mermaid?" Shadow cracked.

Gunner headed outside, pointing both middle fingers back at us until he grabbed the side of the playhouse with a roar.

A sense of relief fell over me as the others went to join him. It had been a tense few moments, but the kids were safe. We were all still here. Trading a rooster for a llama was miles better than a bloody shootout.

I'd take days like this over potentially losing any of them in a heartbeat.

ELEVEN

GUNNER

I came home like any other day, whistling a cheerful tune as I closed the front door behind me. The last thing I expected was a very naked Jandro *leaping* down the stairs toward me.

"Dude, what——"

He clapped a hand over my mouth, the other hand holding a finger to his lips. I noticed he was panting slightly, the skin on his palm felt warm, and his junk swung stiffly at half-mast.

It's not like I was offended by his nudity. Obviously we all shared a wife and a bedroom. Over the years, us guys had become comfortable to the point where catching each other in various states of undress no longer fazed us.

Still, we weren't exactly in the habit of greeting each other at the front door in our birthday suits.

"Don't say a word," Jandro whispered, glancing

over his shoulder toward the bedroom. "I don't think she heard you. But we were just talking about this, and she wants to play a guessing game. You in?"

At my confused expression, he carefully lifted his palm from my mouth. "It's better if you just see her. But remember, not a word. Not even a sound."

I nodded and made the *okay* sign with my hand. Clearly, it was some kind of bedroom game with Mari. She had to be blindfolded or something and that just got my pulse racing with anticipation.

Jandro pressed his finger to his lips once more, and I nodded eagerly while making a shooing motion toward the stairs. He headed that way and I followed right on his heels, just as excited as the kids on Christmas morning.

A scent hit me halfway up the stairs—citrusy, fresh, and warm. My eager smile grew when I realized it was one of those candles Mari loved, the one she said smelled like me.

Jandro and I reached the bedroom and the sight before me was...*holy fuck*. I couldn't have made a sound if I tried, I was that blown away.

Candles flickered on the nightstands, and through the slats of the headboard, Mari's wrists were tied with a soft length of rope. My gaze trailed lower, insistent on not missing any detail. Her arms extended above her were relaxed, a soft bend in her elbows. Mari's dark hair spilled out on the pillows propping up her head and neck for comfort. A black sleep mask covered her eyes, contrasting with the pink flush in her cheeks and lips.

Mari's head rolled from side to side at the sound of our footsteps, her arms tugging lightly at her restraints as her body shifted.

"Jandro? Who came home?" she asked in a tight, breathless voice.

Oh fuck me, did he leave her hanging when he came downstairs? I wanted to slide a glance at him but couldn't take my eyes off of her.

"You're gonna have to guess." Jandro rounded the bed, moving toys and bottles of massage oil out of the way so he could lie next to her. "Isn't that what you wanted?"

Mari's torso stretched out long on the bed, arched with every beautiful, mouthwatering curve on display. Her skin was dewy and flushed, red marks around her waist and breasts as evidence to Jandro's handling.

"Oh, we're playing this already?" A delighted smile pulled at her lips, hips shifting in a way that forced me to swallow down a groan. "Well, I'm going to need some clues."

My eyes hadn't even reached the most tantalizing part, and then I really had to force myself to be quiet. She was spread eagle, ankles tied to the foot of the bed with a little slack for movement. The center of her was so beautifully open and exposed, pussy flushed and glossy with her pleasure.

"Don't leave our poor wife in suspense now."

Jandro dragged the back of his hand up her side, and she startled at the slight touch.

"Jandro, is that you?"

"Yes, it's me." His caress continued up her arm. "Your mystery man is dealing with the loss of blood from his head to his other head."

"I want to know who it is." Mari tugged on her restraints again, hips rising off the bed in a clear invitation. "Shadow, are you going shy on me? Or are you Reaper, thinking of all the ways you'll torture me?"

I'd be tasting blood soon if I kept biting my tongue this hard. But oh, where to begin? She was laid out and tied up so pretty for me, like the most precious gift. Did I just climb on and sink into her like my lizard brain was screaming at me to do? She was already warmed up and ready.

No. I knew the answer the moment my hands went to my belt buckle, pulling everything loose and then off entirely. A woman who presented herself to her men like this deserved to be cherished. Savored. Worshipped.

"Atta boy," Jandro remarked when the last of my clothes came off.

"It *is* Shadow." Mari turned her face to him with a triumphant grin. "You'd only talk to him like that."

"Hmm, are you sure?" He touched a finger to her nose, then dragged the digit to her lips where she sucked it into her mouth. "No biting. You've been such a good girl, I'd hate to ruin it for you now."

While she whined and moaned around his finger, I started my touch at her ankle closest to me. Just a light caress of the soft rope holding her in place before running slowly over her skin.

I followed the curve of her calf muscle, drinking in her shiver as I traveled up to the inside of her knee.

"Hmm, way too gentle to be Reaper," she mused. "So you're either Shadow or Gunner."

I answered by closing my hand in a tight grip of her thigh, just above her knee. Fuck, I never realized before now how much I loved talking to her in bed. This whole silence thing was fucking torture.

"Oh, am I wrong?" Mari smirked under her blindfold. "Kiss me, Reaper."

No, not yet. That might make it too easy for her. I released my grip and spanned my hand wide as I moved it up her thigh. Her breath hitched, hips rising and tilting as I neared her pussy, but I roamed higher to her waist and belly.

"Oh, you're gonna be mean about it, then," she pouted, turning her face toward Jandro again. "Did you tell him to be mean?"

"Just to not say a word." Jandro dragged a hand down her opposite leg. "If it's any consolation, he's having a very difficult time and looks constipated."

Mari laughed, relaxing her head back on the pillows. "This *is* hard."

Jandro snickered. "I can confirm that that is also true."

My patience couldn't hold out forever. After running up to her slender throat, I dragged my hand back down her body, scissoring my fingers open to glide along the sides of her pussy.

Mari gasped, gorgeous lips falling open as she lifted up to press harder against my hand. I almost said something about how sexy and wet she looked, but a tongue click from Jandro reminded me to keep quiet.

Fuck me, I felt muzzled, caged. Being unable to express myself made me feel just as bound as she was. How long would I have to keep this silence up?

My teeth ached with how hard I clenched them, but I kept my touch light as I stroked and explored between her legs. Did Jandro fuck her like this or just use toys on her? How many orgasms did she have before I came home? So many questions I was dying to know but couldn't voice yet.

I crawled onto the bed, carefully stepping over her spread-open legs so I could sit between them.

"Yes, come closer." Mari grinned from under her mask. "Touch me and tell me more about who you are."

"Mean, wicked temptress." Jandro stroked circular patterns over her collarbones and chest. "The poor guy is barely holding it together, and you're not making it any easier for him."

"Maybe you should do a better job of distracting me."

Jandro answered with a growl, his hand closing around her throat before he claimed her mouth in a kiss. Without her taunting me to speak, I could focus for a moment.

I pressed two fingers inside her, watching the resulting arch of her back and her soft gasp through kissing Jandro. My other hand made another roaming pass up her body, rising and dipping as I followed her curves and hypnotic movements. Inside her, my fingers spread and curled, coaxing her slick walls into responding to me. I watched her face while her hips bucked against my hand, keeping my thumb away from her clit for the moment.

Mari broke away from Jandro, panting. A soft moan built up in her throat as she arched and tugged at her restraints.

"Any ideas?" Jandro directed the question at her but grinned at me.

"I'm...fuck, not sure." Her hips tilted from side to side, as if trying to feel my hand from all possible angles. "Feels like...Reaper? Maybe Gunner? I don't know, but it's so good." She sent a coy smile my way, now that her mouth was free. "Whoever you are, I want your cock. Not your hand."

I huffed out a soft laugh, barely more than a breath, but she heard it.

"Oh, what's that?" She cocked her head. "Tell me more."

Fuck. I needed to keep *my* mouth occupied if I

didn't want to break too soon. And what better to feast on than the beautiful dessert spread out in front of me?

I scooted back, leaning down to kiss her hip crease while my fingers continued to drive through her soaked pussy.

"Reaper!" Mari declared when I dragged more kisses toward her core. "It's Reaper."

"Are you *sure?*" Jandro asked.

Mari hesitated. "Fuck, I can't remember if Gunner shaved this morning. His face is usually smoother but, ahh!"

I ran late this morning getting the kids to their swim lessons, so I did not, in fact, have time to shave.

Mari squirmed under the friction of my stubbled jaw, which I dragged along her skin just to tease her now. I'd roast her later for mistaking me for Reaper. She was getting close to figuring it out. Once I sucked that luscious clit into my mouth, angling my fingers inside her to hit that spot that drove her wild, there would be no doubt in her mind.

"Fuck!" She pulled in a sharp gasp, hips bucking desperately into my face. Her moans were smothered after a moment by Jandro kissing her. Or his dick in her mouth, I couldn't exactly see.

I savored every tremble and desperate whine with my tongue, lapping at her and demanding more. I was right at the source, and I wanted all of her pleasure. She came apart within a minute, bursting with sweetness that I couldn't get enough of. Her pussy closed around my fingers like it would never let them go, wetness filling my palm and running to my wrist. I stroked her and drank from her until she shifted away.

My woman was limp, breath sawing in and out of her chest as I crawled over her and leaned down to whisper in her ear, "Hey, baby girl."

Mari's laugh was bright as she licked my cheek. "I knew it was you."

"Uh-huh." I kissed her mouth, her lips so warm and plush, while I slowly settled my weight on top of her. "You sounded pretty convinced I was Reaper."

"Didn't want to bruise your ego. You were trying so hard to be sneaky."

"Mm-hm." I kissed her again, drinking her lips in slowly while I nudged and shifted until my cock notched at her scorching, slick center. "You want to stay tied up?"

"Yeah, I like this." Mari's grin was as bright as sunlight. "But I want to see you."

I lifted the sleeping mask away, watching her gorgeous eyes blink and adjust to the light before settling on me. Her smile grew even bigger and it literally made my heart skip a beat.

Fuck me. Not that there were any doubts that I made the right decision to be hers all those years ago, but it was moments like these that solidified just how right this was.

As time went on, our tentative, fragile relationship

only grew stronger. What started as a weak sapling became an impenetrable oak tree. And our roots grew deep, supporting our children and setting them up for a better future. Not just me, but all of us and Mari were an unbreakable network. One that the gods entrusted to bring humanity back from the brink. What we had was truly endless.

"What?" Mari licked the tip of my nose after I'd been staring at her wondrously for who knows how long.

"Fuck, I just love you."

The goofiness left her face as she gazed up at me. "I love you, Gun."

She tilted her chin up for another kiss, which I happily gave her. Her legs clamped around my waist and I surged forward, every cell in my body aching to be touching her, to be part of her.

The first thrust was the sweetest agony, the exact thing I'd been craving since walking into this room and seeing her tied and spread. Our joint moan was followed by a weight lifting off the bed—Jandro getting up.

"Hey." I lifted up from Mari to look at him. "You don't have to leave."

Beneath me, Mari cackled softly while Jandro gave a sheepish grin, wiping his junk with a towel.

"I'm good, man, I got mine already. We had just, ah..." His teeth sank into his lip, a little embarrassed but also shameless. "Switched places when you got home."

"You mean...?" I looked down at Mari, and the smugness on her face said it all.

"Mm-hm," she confirmed. "I had him tied up first."

"Really?" I lifted my gaze back up to Jandro. "You liked it?"

"More than I thought I would." He waved a hand at us as he turned away. "Tell you about it later. I'm gonna shower. You kids have fun."

I returned my full attention to the woman laughing quietly underneath me. Her chuckles stretched out into moans as I sank down to her and *into* her.

"You know, *I* wouldn't mind being tied up." I dragged through her long and slow, savoring every inch of bliss and wanting to make it last.

"Oh, really?" Mari looked thoroughly pleased at that idea. "I can see you tied to a chair. Makes for a very pretty picture in my mind." She tugged at her wrist bindings, as if already eager to transfer the rope to my hands.

I slid my arms under her arched back to hold her closer. "What would you do to me?"

"Hmm—ah!" Her head threw back at my next thrust going deeper, a little harder. The bare column of her throat was so sexy, I couldn't help but take a nibble.

"Tell me or you don't get to come." I pulled away with another long drag from her silky heat.

Her gaze snapped back to me with a soft bark of a laugh. "Ha. I'd shove a gag in that smart mouth first so your talking doesn't distract me."

"Aw, but don't you love it when I talk to you?" I rolled forward again, sinking deep into her pussy while my fist closed in her hair. My hips snapped harder as I brought my mouth to her ear. "Wouldn't you want to hear me beg for this pussy? Beg you to climb on and fuck me?"

"You'd try to get out of being tied up first," she said, her breaths coming in harsher as she absorbed the impact of my thrusts.

"You mean there's a chance I'd succeed?" I sucked along the crook of her neck and her shoulder, our skin sliding and bodies flush.

"I'd let you think there was."

"Mean," I grunted.

We laughed at the same time and our lips found each other again. I slid a hand up to clasp with one of hers as we rocked together. My thrusts grew wild as I got greedier for more of her moans and rough breaths, more of the sweet pressure wrapping around all sides of my cock.

Mari came once more with a muffled cry through a kiss and a tight squeeze around my length that had me tumbling right after her. I'd been wound up like a spring since I first walked into the room, and now it spilled out of me in a dizzying rush.

I was limp on top of her, all frayed nerves and a drumming heartbeat. My face pressed into the pillow next to Mari's head, ready to fall asleep in that position if I hadn't felt her nip on my ear.

"Untie me now, please," she whispered, all sated and relaxed.

"Nah, I like you like this."

Mari's huff tickled my cheek, and I pressed lazy kisses to her face until she laughed, then sat up to untie her.

"We'll use these on you next time," she said, playfully whipping me with one of the ends of the ropes. "Jury's still out on if I'll have to gag you."

"What if I promised to be a good boy?" I caressed down her legs before plucking the knots that held her ankles.

"I'd call you a liar."

She started to sit up, but I pounced on her and pinned her back down to the bed. My attack of kisses and tickling filled the room with laughter and echoed throughout the house.

TWELVE

REAPER

I slid across the open, expansive mattress until I reached her. My arm fit perfectly around her waist, and she left enough room on the pillow for me to lay my head just behind hers. It was rare that we ended up in bed together alone, and I wanted to bask in it.

Mari stirred, stretching out long with a soft groan before she laced her fingers with mine. "You're not on breakfast duty?" she asked sleepily.

"Nah. Daren wanted Gunner's pancakes, so he pounced on him. And Rori wanted Shadow to make orange juice with her, so she got him up." I squeezed around her waist, nuzzling her cheek. "You slept through all that? It was a fucking racket in here for a minute."

"Long night at the hospital, we had an emergency

C-section," she mumbled, then elbowed me lazily. "You know I sleep like the dead anyway."

"Never fails to amaze me, what you sleep through," I chuckled into her hair. "Everything turn out okay at the hospital?"

"Oh yeah, everything was fine. Triplets." She elbowed me again. "Three *big* boys."

"There's Rori's future harem."

"No, don't," Mari pleaded. "They're growing so fast. I don't want to think about her as a woman yet."

I laughed into her hair, a question on the tip of my tongue. One that we'd danced around, brought up in passing, but never had a chance to really discuss before now.

"Sugar." I wrapped tighter around her, bringing her back flush to my chest. "Do you want to have any more?"

Mari turned her head, looking at me over her shoulder. "More kids?"

"Yeah."

She rolled slowly, turning over to face me. We lied next to each other nose-to-nose, her arm settling over my shoulder with her fingers stroking lightly over my back.

"I think we could handle another one or two more." Caution tinged her voice, and she didn't exactly look overjoyed.

"But do you *want* more?" I asked.

"I don't want to carry twins again," she admitted.

"I'm glad we got Rori and Daren at the same time, but even though everything turned out fine, that was fucking rough. Even with all you guys to help."

"What are the chances of that happening again?"

"I don't know. Greater than zero," she chuckled. "It already happened once."

"True."

We were quiet for a few moments while she nuzzled her head under my chin. "If we do try again, it should probably be soon," she said in my chest. "Before the twins get much older."

I stroked down the length of hair covering her back. "None of us *need* more kids. The twins are perfect. They're the center of our universe, and all of us would be happy keeping it that way. Our life is perfect, sugar. Nothing needs to change if we don't want it to."

Mari sighed against my skin. "If I was almost certain I could have one at a time, I wouldn't hesitate to say yes. But so many women are having multiple births right now. There's some kind of baby boom going on and none of the doctors can figure what's causing it."

"You think it's Freyja's doing?" I wondered aloud.

"She's involved, I'm sure." Mari lifted her head to look at the cat, curled up and sleeping at the foot of the bed.

"She looked after you during your pregnancy, right?"

"They all did," Mari said with a soft smile. "She'd rub on me when the aches were the worst. Hades never let any strangers get near me. Even Horus screeched his head off when that missionary came over, remember?"

"He did a full-on hunting dive, then pulled back at the last second." I laughed at the memory. "Poor guy almost got his neck flayed open."

"Even with all that," Mari waved her hand in the air. "Pregnancy with twins is not something I'm dying to repeat."

"I get it, sugar."

"It's like," she leaned away from me, chewing her lip, "I never got to *know* them until they were born. They kept switching places, flipping around inside me. I never knew if it was Rory kicking the shit out of me or Daren."

"Well, *now* we know who the little shit-kicker was," I grumbled. Rori got me hard in the balls one time during a tantrum, to the point where I had to sit with a bag of ice on my crotch for a few hours.

"Right." Mari laughed. "But me bonding with them during pregnancy is different, I think. If I have one baby in there, I can learn about them before they're born. What kind of food or music they like, what times they're sleepy or active. I'd like to experience that, instead of wondering who's beating up my insides this time."

"That sounds nice," I said, already picturing her

with a round belly again. "Too bad dads can't experience that firsthand."

Mari laughed so hard she woke up Freyja. The cat blinked at us with a narrow-eyed glare before turning to sleep in another position.

"Yes, such a shame men can't experience the joy of pregnancy," Mari said in a dry tone. "The world would be very different if they could."

"Yeah, well. Not the way it works." I pulled her back toward me until we were intertwined again—her head on my chest, our arms in a tangled embrace, and her leg over my hip. "If you want to try again, we're ready," I murmured into her hairline.

"Course you are," Mari chuckled, bringing a hand to my jaw. "I want one that looks like you," she added softly.

That statement took my breath away, and my overfilled well of love for this woman spilled over a little more.

"If we have another boy, can we name him Nolan?" I asked.

Mari nudged her nose against mine with a smile. "I'd love that. But Finn's going to get jealous."

"Finn can get the middle name," I huffed. "But no, he'll actually love it. You remember how he cried when we said our son would be Daren? He's overjoyed that we're remembering the ones we lost this way."

"What about if we have a girl?" Mari stuck her

tongue out to the tip of my nose, but little did she know I'd been thinking about that too.

"Lucia," I said softly.

Mari blinked, taken aback. "After Jandro's mom."

"Yeah. What do you think?"

Jandro didn't show it much, but we could all tell the lack of information on his missing parents weighed heavily on him. He and sisters got in touch with agencies looking to reunite family members across Mexico and the Southwest, but their searches turned up next to nothing. His aunt and uncle would be moving up here next year and his sisters visited regularly, but that big question mark regarding his parents had to be a sore spot.

We might never get answers. Such was the nature of the Collapse.

"That's beautiful." Mari smiled a bit wistfully. "Make sure it's okay with Jandro though."

"I know, it's a family decision." I moved a lock of hair from her shoulder. "He seems to have…accepted the most likely outcome, so I thought it might be nice. And it's a pretty name."

"It is." Mari rolled away and stretched long with a yawn. "Alright, what do you say, Freyja?" She poked the disgruntled, half-asleep cat with her foot. "I'll have more babies, but give 'em to me one at a time, okay?"

If you insist.

The two of us froze and then looked at each other.

"Was that…?"

"I think so."

A wave of amusement passed over me, like the vibrations of someone's laughter on my skin. It brought a grin to my face and Mari looked just as giddy.

"Is that enough confirmation for you?" I reached for her, blatantly groping and pawing to pull her closer.

"I think it's the only one I'm getting." She sounded excited and nervous, her beautiful grin infectious.

"Then what are we waiting for?" I brought my wife underneath me, settling between her thighs as I leaned down to kiss her, only to be stopped by an impressively loud rumbling from her stomach.

"Breakfast." Mari laughed. "I need fuel if I'm gonna get knocked up again."

"Fine." I sighed, but lowered to kiss her anyway. "You'll be fed." I kissed her nose bridge. "Protected." Her forehead. "Adored." Her right eye. "Cherished." Her left eye. "Loved. For the rest of my days."

I sealed every promise with a kiss. Ones she knew and that I didn't need to repeat, but liked to do so anyway.

"You really can be sweet sometimes," she said, eyes glittering.

"You make it easy sometimes."

I earned another lick on my nose for that, then

hauled her upright with more kisses and laughter. There was a new excitement buzzing in our touches and smiles. It matched the bright giddiness in my chest and I couldn't wait to tell everyone downstairs.

We had breakfast to eat and then more babies to make.

THE END

———

Can't get enough of Shadow?

From the Shadows contains three bonus scenes from Shadow's POV not included in the original Steel Demons series.

Grab it for free here when you sign up for my newsletter!

———

Want to know what happened to the Sons of Odin? Their book is available now!
Click to start reading Their Property!

———

Ready for the next generation?
Faithless: Book 1 of Vengeful Gods MC releases
December 2022!

PRE-ORDER FAITHLESS HERE:

https://books2read.com/VGMC1

Acknowledgments

I wrote my long, sappy Acknowledgements page at the end of Merciless, so I'll spare you all this time!

If you've made it this far, simply thank you. I appreciate you more than words can say. You're part of the global Steel Demons family, and you matter to *me*. Thank you for letting my story take you on a ride.

The Steel Demons' story is finished, but who knows? We just might see them again one day…

When one ride is over, another begins! For regular updates, exclusive teasers, and excerpts, join my reader group, Crystal's Coven.

See you all in the next book!

-Crystal

Also by Crystal Ash

Harem of Freaks: The Complete Series

Say Your Prayers

Steel Demons MC

Lawless

Powerless

Fearless

Painless

Helpless

Heartless

Senseless

Ruthless

Merciless

Endless

Their Property: Sons of Odin MC

Shifted Mates Trilogy

Unholy Trinity: The Complete Series

For a complete list of books by Crystal Ash, visit her Amazon page.

About the Author

Crystal Ash is a USA Today Bestselling Author from California. She loves writing steamy, heart-wrenching romance with tortured heroes, especially if they're in a reverse harem. Crystal's other loves include animals, mythology, and well-crafted alcohol, most of which can also be found in her stories.

When she's not writing, she's probably drinking craft beer with her husband or trying to coax her feral cat into accepting affection.

crystalashbooks.com

facebook.com/Crystal.Ash.Romance

instagram.com/crystalashbooks

amazon.com/author/crystalash

bookbub.com/profile/crystal-ash

www.ingramcontent.com/pod-product-compliance
Lightning Source LLC
Chambersburg PA
CBHW051232210726
48290CB00003B/914